Erle Stanley Gardner and The Murder Room

>>> This title is part of The Murder Room, our series dedicated to making available out-of-print or hard-to-find titles by classic crime writers.

Crime fiction has always held up a mirror to society. The Victorians were fascinated by sensational murder and the emerging science of detection; now we are obsessed with the forensic detail of violent death. And no other genre has so captivated and enthralled readers.

Vast troves of classic crime writing have for a long time been unavailable to all but the most dedicated frequenters of second-hand bookshops. The advent of digital publishing means that we are now able to bring you the backlists of a huge range of titles by classic and contemporary crime writers, some of which have been out of print for decades.

From the genteel amateur private eyes of the Golden Age and the femmes fatales of pulp fiction, to the morally ambiguous hard-boiled detectives of mid twentieth-century America and their descendants who walk our twenty-first century streets, The Murder Room has it all. >>>

The Murder Room
Where Criminal Minds Meet

themurderroom.com

Erle Stanley Gardner (1889–1970)

Born in Malden, Massachusetts, Erle Stanley Gardner left school in 1909 and attended Valparaiso University School of Law in Indiana for just one month before he was suspended for focusing more on his hobby of boxing that his academic studies. Soon after, he settled in California, where he taught himself the law and passed the state bar exam in 1911. The practise of law never held much interest for him, however, apart from as it pertained to trial strategy, and in his spare time he began to write for the pulp magazines that gave Dashiell Hammett and Raymond Chandler their start. Not long after the publication of his first novel, *The Case of the Velvet Claws*, featuring Perry Mason, he gave up his legal practice to write full time. He had one daughter, Grace, with his first wife, Natalie, from whom he later separated. In 1968 Gardner married his long-term secretary, Agnes Jean Bethell, whom he professed to be the real 'Della Street', Perry Mason's sole (although unacknowledged) love interest. He was one of the most successful authors of all time and at the time of his death, in Temecula, California in 1970, is said to have had 135 million copies of his books in print in America alone.

By *Erle Stanley Gardner*
(titles below include only those
published in the Murder Room)

Perry Mason series

The Case of the Sulky Girl
(1933)

The Case of the Baited Hook
(1940)

The Case of the Borrowed
Brunette (1946)

The Case of the Lonely
Heiress (1948)

The Case of the Negligent
Nymph (1950)

The Case of the Moth-Eaten
Mink (1952)

The Case of the Glamorous
Ghost (1955)

The Case of the Terrified
Typist (1956)

The Case of the Gilded Lily
(1956)

The Case of the Lucky Loser
(1957)

The Case of the Long-Legged
Models (1958)

The Case of the Deadly Toy
(1959)

The Case of the Singing Skirt
(1959)

The Case of the Duplicate
Daughter (1960)

The Case of the Blonde
Bonanza (1962)

Cool and Lam series

*First published under the
pseudonym A. A. Fair*

The Bigger They Come (1939)

Turn on the Heat (1940)

Gold Comes in Bricks (1940)

Spill the Jackpot (1941)

Double or Quits (1941)

Owls Don't Blink (1942)

Bats Fly at Dusk (1942)

Cats Prowl at Night (1943)

Crows Can't Count (1946)

Fools Die on Friday (1947)

Bedrooms Have Windows
(1949)

Some Women Won't Wait (1953)

Beware the Curves (1956)

You Can Die Laughing (1957)

Some Slips Don't Show (1957)

The Count of Nine (1958)

Pass the Gravy (1959)

Kept Women Can't Quit (1960)

Bachelors Get Lonely (1961)
Shills Can't Count Chips (1961)
Try Anything Once (1962)
Fish or Cut Bait (1963)
Up For Grabs (1964)
Cut Thin to Win (1965)
Widows Wear Weeds (1966)
Traps Need Fresh Bait (1967)

Doug Selby D.A. series

The D.A. Calls it Murder (1937)
The D.A. Holds a Candle (1938)
The D.A. Draws a Circle (1939)
The D.A. Goes to Trial (1940)
The D.A. Cooks a Goose (1942)
The D.A. Calls a Turn (1944)

The D.A. Takes a Chance (1946)
The D.A. Breaks an Egg (1949)

Terry Clane series

Murder Up My Sleeve (1937)
The Case of the Backward
   Mule (1946)

Gramp Wiggins series

The Case of the Turning Tide
   (1941)
The Case of the Smoking
   Chimney (1943)

Two Clues (two novellas) (1947)

Up For Grabs

Erle Stanley Gardner

An Orion book

Copyright © The Erle Stanley Gardner Trust 1964

This edition published by
The Orion Publishing Group Ltd
Orion House
5 Upper St Martin's Lane
London WC2H 9EA

An Hachette UK company
A CIP catalogue record for this book is available from the British Library

ISBN 978 1 4719 0920 7

www.orionbooks.co.uk

Chapter 1

Elsie Brand, my secretary, jumped up from her chair as I opened the door.

"Donald," she said, "Bertha's having kittens!"

"Again?"

"She's *really* running a temperature this time."

"What's the trouble?"

"A new contact. The man is a big executive and won't wait. They have to talk with you."

"Give her a ring," I said. "Tell her I'm here."

"No, no, you're to go in just as soon as you come. She's given me instructions."

"Who is this executive? Do you know?"

"He's very distinguished looking," she said. "Looks like a banker or a very rich broker."

"Okay," I said. "I'll go take a look."

I walked out of my office, crossed the main reception room to the door which said: B. COOL—PRIVATE.

The "B" stood for Bertha, and Bertha stood for 165 pounds of belligerency, diamond-hard eyes, a figure that had sagged into a cylinder, bulldog jaw, and a face that ran somewhat to jowls unless she held her chin up and sucked her cheeks in, which she did whenever she wanted to look really impressive.

Bertha Cool's eyes glittered at me. "Well, it's about time *you* got here! Where have you been?"

"Working on a case," I said.

"Shake hands with Mr. Breckinridge," she said. "He's been waiting nearly twenty minutes."

"How are you, Mr. Breckinridge?" I said.

The guy stood up. He was tall, slim-waisted, grizzled, forty-five or so, with a close-cropped gray mustache and quizzical gray eyes. He was a little over six feet, which put him a good six inches above me, and from the tan on his face, running uniformly up his forehead, it was a cinch he was a golf addict.

Bertha said, "Mr. Breckinridge is the head of the All Purpose Insurance Company. He's looking for a private detective who can do a highly specialized job. He thinks you are the man for the job."

Breckinridge smiled, a toothy flash of instant cordiality. "I had a pretty good lead on you before I came over here, Lam. I've looked you up rather carefully."

I didn't say anything.

Bertha Cool's chair creaked under her weight. She said to Breckinridge, "You want to tell him or shall I?"

"I'll tell him," Breckinridge said.

"Okay," Bertha said in a voice which indicated she thought she could do it better but was yielding to an important client as a matter of courtesy.

Breckinridge said, "Have one of my cards, Lam."

2

He gave me a handsomely embossed card which showed that his first name was Homer; that he was the president and general manager of the All Purpose Insurance Company.

Breckinridge said, "We need someone who differs from the average for our work. Most clients want a private detective who is on the beefy side. *We* need someone who is young, alert, and accustomed to using brains instead of brawn. We have steady, lucrative work for such a man."

"Donald's your man," Bertha said, the chair creaking again as she turned toward Breckinridge.

"I think so," Breckinridge said.

"Now, wait a minute," Bertha said, suddenly suspicious, "you aren't trying to hire him away from the partnership?"

"No, no," Breckinridge said, "that's precisely why I'm here, but I am convinced we're going to have quite a bit of work for Mr. Lam."

"Fifty bucks a day and expenses—take all you want," Bertha said. "Those are our rates."

"Fair enough," Breckinridge said. "We'll pay sixty."

"What's the pitch?" I asked.

Breckinridge said, somewhat unctuously, "Standards of honesty in this country seem to be undergoing a steady deterioration, a progressive disintegration."

No one said anything to that.

"In the insurance business," Breckinridge went on, "we find we are dealing more and more frequently with chiselers, malingerers, people who magnify their injuries beyond all reason.

"And," he went on, warming to his subject, "we find an increasing number of attorneys who have made a careful study of how to influence susceptible jurors so that physical pain and suffering have now been distorted out of all proportion to reality.

"Let a man have a simple backache, and an attorney stands up in front of the jurors and tells them there are twenty-four hours in a day, that there are sixty minutes in each hour, and sixty seconds in each minute, that his client is suffering agonizing pain every second of every minute of every hour."

Bertha said dryly, "We know *all* the rackets up here —and have worked out procedures to cope with most of them."

"Pardon me," Breckinridge apologized. "I forgot for the moment that I was dealing with professionals and not amateurs.

"Very well, here's the situation in a nutshell. We are now dealing with a man whom we are satisfied is a malingerer. He was involved in an automobile accident and, confidentially, we are going to have to admit liability. Our client has told us he was in the wrong and the evidence will so show.

"The malingerer, a man named Helmann Bruno, resides in Dallas, Texas. He claims a whiplash injury and he has sufficient knowledge to report all the symptoms that go with a whiplash injury of the cervical vertebrae.

"Now, of course, I don't need to explain to you that this is one of the most prolific fields of malingering we have. You can't take an X ray of a headache. You can't deny that, in genuine cases of whiplash injury, the pain may be severe and the injury may be deep-seated and long-lasting.

"On the other hand, you can't find any outward manifestations which can be shown on X rays which conclusively indicate whiplash when they are present, and conclusively indicate malingering when they are absent."

"Just how serious is a whiplash injury?" Bertha asked. "I have heard they can do a lot of damage."

"They can," Breckinridge admitted. "Of course, you get a whiplash injury when the head is violently thrown back causing severe damage to the nerves in the neck.

"These injuries usually take place when a person is sitting in an automobile and someone hits from behind, pushing the automobile forward before the occupant can tighten his neck muscles sufficiently to keep the head from being thrown back, with perhaps resulting damage to the cervical vertebrae, the cranial nerves and—"

Bertha made an impatient gesture by way of interruption. "We know all about how whiplash injuries occur," she said, "but what I wanted to find out was how they were regarded by insurance people and just what could happen once a whiplash injury has been established."

Breckinridge sighed and said, "From an insurance standpoint, Mrs. Cool, once a whiplash injury has been established, almost anything can happen."

Breckinridge turned to me and said, "This is where you come in, Lam."

I said, "Don't you fellows have a pretty good system for exposing malingerers?"

"Of course we do, and you are going to be part of it."

I dropped into a chair and settled back.

Breckinridge said, "When one of these malingerers gets in front of a jury, he's sick; he's oh, so sick; he moans and groans; he looks wan and pathetic; his eloquent attorney draws charts, and a jury awards lots of damages on the theory that, after all, the insurance company charges ample premiums for its policies and can well afford the liability.

"Experience has shown, however, that even in the worst of these cases, after we make a settlement with the injured, there is nearly always a remarkable recovery; particularly, with nervous injuries. In some instances the recovery is simply miraculous. People who have the sworn testimony of doctors that they are permanently injured go out on a camping trip within twenty-four hours after the settlement is made or take an excursion on a boat, where they become the life of the party.

"Now, of course, this rat race is not entirely one-sided. We have worked out a technique of our own. We trap these people into a situation where it is to their advantage to become active and alert, then we get motion pictures of them. In court, after a man has testified that he can hardly lift his hands as high as his shoulders, that he can only walk by taking short, faltering steps, we show pictures of him diving off a springboard, playing tennis, and swinging golf clubs.

"Now obviously, that takes some doing and, strangely enough, juries don't like it."

"What do you mean they don't like it?" Bertha asked.

"They feel we've been spying on the guy, intruding on his privacy— Good heavens, why shouldn't we intrude on his privacy or do anything else that is required under the circumstances?"

"But the juries don't like it?" I reminded him.

He stroked the angle of his chin, let the tips of his fingers smooth his stubby mustache and said, "They don't like the entrapment."

There was a moment of silence.

"You don't mean you've given up taking these motion pictures?" I asked.

"Not at all. Not at all," he said. "We've simply decided to change the approach so that we appear to a little better advantage in front of a jury.

"Now, that is where you come in, Lam.

"To take the pictures, we usually have had a camper body mounted on a pickup, or a van with apertures cut in the sides. We trap a man into playing golf, for instance, and have a concealed camera where we can get pictures of him making practice swings, and things like that.

"Then when he says he can't use his arms without

pain, we show motion pictures of him whipping a golf club in an arc.

"Well, the jurors don't like it. They feel we've trapped the fellow. They'll cut their verdicts down all right, but they are left with a feeling of antagonism toward the insurance carrier.

"So now we have worked out certain refinements which we feel will improve our public relations."

"Go ahead," Bertha said.

"Well now, for instance, we'll start with Helmann Bruno," Breckinridge said. "He's married but has no children. He has his own business, a manufacturer's agency, which keeps him on the road quite a bit of the time.

"So we laid a trap for Mr. Helmann Bruno, because our adjuster sized him up as a phony right from the start."

"What did you do?" Bertha asked.

"This, of course, is confidential," Breckinridge said.

Bertha's diamonds glittered as she swept her hand in an inclusive circular gesture. "Within the four walls of the office," she promised.

"Well," Breckinridge said, "we had some circulars printed about a so-called contest. The contest is so absurdly easy a man can't resist taking a fling. He is supposed to tell in fifty words or less why he likes a certain product. We send a printed business envelope and a blank so that all the man has to do when he receives our letter is sit there for a moment, write fifty words, stick the message in the envelope and the envelope in the mail. He can't possibly lose anything and he stands a chance of winning all sorts of glittering prizes."

"Who pays for this contest and who judges it?" Bertha asked.

Breckinridge grinned. "The contest has a *very* limited mailing list, Mrs. Cool. Actually, we send it out only to persons who are making false claims against the company and every one of those persons who replies wins a prize."

Bertha's eyebrows came up.

"The prize which the man wins," Breckinridge said, "will always be the same. We'll send him to the Butte Valley Guest Ranch at Tucson, Arizona."

"Why this particular dude ranch?" I asked.

"Because the hostess, Dolores Ferrol, is under retainer from us; because the routine is such that a person who doesn't do horseback riding is very much out of things during the morning, and if he doesn't swim, play golf or volleyball in the afternoon, he's not going to enjoy himself.

"The 'dudes' return from a morning horseback ride tired and dusty; the swimming pool is cool and inviting; lunch is served by the pool.

"Now then, we had originally planned to have our detectives all ready to entice this malingerer into the communal activities.

"Jurors won't like that. We'd have to put our man on the stand and ask him his name and his occupation and he'd say he was in our employ as a detective and then go on and tell what had happened and show motion pictures of the guy doing high dives, playing golf and riding horseback.

"Then the attorney for the plaintiff would take him on cross-examination and some of those attorneys are remarkably clever. They couldn't talk much about their client because the photographs would show that we had the deadwood on him, but they'd start talking about the witness. They'd say, 'You are in the employ of the All Purpose Insurance Company?'

" 'That's right.'

" 'And you went down there with the deliberate intention of luring this plaintiff into all sorts of physical activities so that he could be photographed.'

" 'Yes, sir.'

" 'And the insurance company paid all your expenses and paid you a salary to boot. And you expect they're going to keep on paying you a salary as long as your services are satisfactory?'

" 'Yes, sir.'

" 'And you went down there intending to lure this plaintiff into a trap before you had ever seen him?'

" 'That's right.'

" 'You didn't know the nature and extent of his injuries. You didn't know how much pain it caused him to try and be a good fellow. You deliberately prodded him into all of these athletic activities. You professed a friendship for him. You had no consideration whatever for the pain and anguish which tortured his injured body. Your only purpose was to get the photographs which you could show this jury. Isn't that right?' "

Breckinridge threw out his hands. "Well, of course that sinks the plaintiff's case as far as really big judgments against us are concerned, but the sympathies of the jurors are with the plaintiff still. They feel that we played dirty pool. The jurors give him a sort of consolation prize. We don't like that feeling; it's bad public relations. We want to educate jurors so they'll feel that the malingerer is a dirty, chiseling crook.

"Now then, Lam, that's where you come in. Helmann Bruno has already fallen for this contest business. He sent in fifty words and we advised him by wire—using the name of the dummy corporation that conducts the contest, of course—that he had won a two-week, all-expense trip to the Butte Valley Guest Ranch."

"What about his wife?" I asked.

Breckinridge laughed. "He didn't say anything about his wife and we didn't—the malingerer never does. The chiseler always leaves his wife at home.

"If a guy would write in and say, 'It's all right, boys, I've won a prize for two weeks free at this dude ranch, but I'm a married man; now, can I have my wife with me and cut the time to one week?' We'd say, 'Sure' and we'd make a settlement with him right then, because that guy wouldn't be a chiseler. But the married men who decide they're going to make some excuse to their wives about being away on business, and instead go to this expensive dude ranch without their wives, are the chiselers. They're the malingerers. They're the cheap, petty crooks. They're the philanderers.

"Now then, Lam, we want you to go to the Butte Valley Guest Ranch. Dolores Ferrol will take you under her wing just as soon as you get there. She'll see that you have every opportunity to enjoy yourself and get everything you want.

"As far as expenses are concerned, the sky's the limit. Spend anything that you think is necessary in order to get results.

"Now, the first thing you'll need is a feminine inspiration."

"I can take someone with me?" I asked hopefully.

"Definitely not," Breckinridge said. "That's where we've made our mistakes before. We've had a couple go there, and the plaintiff's attorneys have put them on the defensive right away."

"How come?" Bertha asked.

"Well, if they're married," Breckinridge said, "the counsel takes the witnesses on cross-examination and says, in effect, *'You deliberately used your wife as bait in order to get this guy in the position you wanted him, didn't you?'*

"And if they aren't married, the attorney says, 'Oh, you were there for two weeks with a woman who was not your wife. You had separate sleeping quarters, of course—or did you?'

"If the guy says, yes, they had separate sleeping quarters, then the attorney says, sneeringly, 'You went there together, you stayed there together, you returned home together, and you slept at opposite ends of the dude ranch, did you? Just how far were your rooms separated? As much as a hundred yards? As much as fifty yards?' And then he'll make some sneering remark like 'A sprinter can cover fifty yards in five seconds. How long did it take you?'

"No, we want the detective to keep in the background just as much as possible. You'll get acquainted with some unattached girl who's there, and then see that the malingerer is included in the group and he's given just enough of an element of rivalry so the malingerer wants to start showing off. He shows how strong he is, how masculine he is, how athletic he is."

"And that's all recorded in motion pictures?" I asked.

"That's recorded in motion pictures," Breckinridge said.

"When we shoot those pictures, we keep the detective in the background as much as possible. We emphasize that the young woman was one who was there spending her vacation and that this malingerer was trying to show off in front of her. The jurors won't mind that. They'll get a kick out of it. They won't feel that it's such a frame-up.

"Of course, it may come out on cross-examination that *you* were in our employ, but only as an observer. You didn't bait any traps. You were only watching. Moreover, if we're at all lucky we won't use you at all. We'll keep you off the stand and rely on the testimony of others, the ones whose names you'll furnish."

"How about the girl?" I asked.

13

"Well," Breckinridge said, "we'll keep her in the background as much as possible. We use a long focal-length lens and we narrow the field so the jurors just get a glimpse of the girl and then we have this fellow showing off. If we can get a girl somewhere in her twenties and have a man ten to fifteen years older, trying to make the grade—well, the jurors just say to themselves, 'Why that old fuddy-duddy, who does he think *he's* fooling?'"

"You've had success with that technique?"

"We're just starting with it, Lam, but we know juror psychology. This variation will work like a charm. If we're lucky we can keep you in the background. You'll never have to take the witness stand.

"This approach will break the hearts of the plaintiffs' attorneys who handle these cases on a contingency basis and figure that they can spellbind a jury into bringing in a verdict for ten or fifteen thousand dollars as consolation prizes even in cases where the proof goes against them."

"You'd better tell me the facts about this Helmann Bruno case," I said.

"I've told you, Lam, we've got to admit liability, although of course the plaintiff doesn't know it, and his attorney doesn't know it as yet. In fact he may not even have a lawyer yet.

"Foley Chester, our insured, has an importing business here. He travels rather extensively, part of the time by air, part of the time by automobile. He had a trip to make to Texas and drove to El Paso and transacted some business that he had there and he then drove on to Dallas. While he was in Dallas, he was driving along in a string of traffic, things seemed to be going along all right, he took his eyes off the road ahead momentarily, because an article in a shopwindow interested him, and when he glanced back he saw that the car ahead of him had stopped and he was right on top of it. He slammed on his brakes but hit the automobile.

"Now the point is, the cars were hardly damaged at all. The bumpers absorbed the shock, but his Helmann Bruno *claims* that his head snapped back, that he had a peculiar dizzy feeling but didn't think too much of it.

"Chester and Bruno exchanged addresses, and Bruno said he didn't think he was hurt but he thought he should see a doctor, and Chester told him, by all means, to see a doctor.

"Then Chester went on, the damned fool, to tell him that he was very sorry, that he'd taken his eyes off the road for just a second.

"Well, of course, we've claimed that Bruno brought his car to a stop without giving an adequate stop signal, that he stopped suddenly and without good cause, and all that. But the fact remains that we don't know whether he gave a stop signal or not. His brake lights were working and, for all Chester can tell us, the guy had been stopped as much as a hundred feet ahead of him. Chester was looking to one side and just kept driving along. He plowed right into Bruno—one of those things that sometimes happens."

"And what about the injuries?"

"Well, for a couple of days nothing happened, then Bruno changed doctors. The first doctor said he didn't think there was anything wrong, but the second doctor was a different breed of cat. He found everything wrong. He diagnosed a whiplash injury and put the guy to bed, hired private nurses around the clock, administered sedatives, and all of that stuff.

"By this time, Bruno was educated and was complaining of headaches and dizziness, loss of appetite and all the rest of it."

"Did he actually lose his appetite?"

Breckinridge shrugged his shoulders and said, "A man would miss a lot of meals for fifty thousand dollars."

"Fifty thousand?" I asked.

"That's what he says he's going to sue us for."

"What'll he settle for?"

"Oh, he'd probably settle for ten, but the point is, Lam, we aren't going to pay it. We used to settle these cases but making settlements in cases of this sort is simply an invitation to every lawyer in the country to come rushing in with a so-called whiplash injury case every time anybody scratches paint on a client's car."

"All right," I said, "just what do you want me to do?"

"Pack your bags, take a plane to Tucson, go to the Butte Valley Guest Ranch, put yourself in the hands of Dolores Ferrol. She'll see that you meet Bruno when he arrives, and she'll see that you meet some cute little thing that's either on the make or just spending a two-week vacation and would like to have somebody pay her attention.

"You bring Bruno into the party and make just enough of a play for the girl so it establishes a rivalry.

"That's why we want a detective who is—I mean who isn't— Well, we don't want one who is too big and strong and husky, physically. We want one who is personable and has the ability to make women like him, but one who isn't exactly athletic."

"You can't hurt his feelings," Bertha said. "You want a little cuss, brainy but little."

"No, no," Breckinridge said hastily, "not little but just— Well, we don't want a big coarse, beefy individual, because the malingerer will try to emphasize the qualities he has that his potential rival doesn't have. If he can't match brains with him, he'll move over into the field of brawn.

"That's where we come in."

"How long do I stay?" I asked. "Do I leave when you get the pictures?"

"No," Breckinridge said, "you stay a full three weeks. Bruno will be staying two weeks. You get there first, and you stay after he leaves. You get everything you can on him. We want to find out all we can about his character, his background, his likes and dislikes."

I said, "Okay, I'll do it on one condition."

"What do you mean, one condition?" Bertha Cool snapped. "He's paying our rates."

"What's the condition?" Breckinridge asked.

"I'm not going to make a play for some girl and then put her in an embarrassing position. If I can handle things so it appears Bruno is just showing off generally, that's one thing, but I'm not going to let some girl have her name get dragged into court."

"I don't think I like that," Breckinridge said.

"Neither do I," Bertha chimed in.

"Then go get another detective," I told Breckinridge.

Breckinridge's face flushed. "We *can't* get anybody else. Most of the private detectives run to beef and when we use our own men we antagonize the jurors."

Bertha glowered at me.

It was a good time to keep silent.

I kept silent.

"Okay," Breckinridge said at length, "you win, but I want you to do a good job of it. There's a lot of future work along these lines, and our company isn't a bad company to work for.

"We've decided that it's bad public relations to have our own detectives making a setup of this sort. For the reasons I've pointed out, jurors don't like that. But if we hire an outside detective on a regular basis, the jurors won't mind it as much, and if we can keep this detective in the background, the jurors won't mind it at all. It's when the detective is on our payroll and makes his living doing this sort of thing that the jurors don't like it.

"And using a regular female operative is bad. I don't mind telling you in strict confidence that in the last two

18

cases the cross-examining attorney was able to establish that the pair had been more intimate than the necessities of the situation called for.

"The attorney for the plaintiff quit talking about his client and bore down on our detective furtively slipping through the shadows between the cabins, and then asked him if he got paid time and a half for overtime. It brought down the house.

"We don't want any more cases like that."

"When do I start?" I asked.

"This afternoon," he said. "Get established at this dude ranch. You phone them telling them the plane you're taking and they'll meet you."

"Okay," I said, "I'll pack up my bags and get a reservation on the earliest plane."

Breckinridge said, "I have already made financial arrangements with Mrs. Cool and left her my check."

I saw him to the door and bowed him out.

When I came back, Bertha was beaming. "*This* is the kind of work that's respectable, safe and conservative," she said. "We can make money on this sort of stuff."

"Haven't we been making money?" I asked.

"We've made money," Bertha admitted, "but we've done it skating on thin ice over the brink of Niagara Falls blindfolded. From now on this agency is going to be employed by established corporations, well-heeled insurance companies. The expenses will be paid by the clients as they are incurred. We won't be gambling a cent.

"Here's a whole new portfolio of legitimate insurance business and it's up for grabs. Let's be damned certain we're the ones who grab it and hang on to it."

Chapter 2

It was late afternoon when the plane eased into a landing at Tucson.

I crossed over to the gate and noticed a tall blond individual, somewhere in his early thirties, wearing a cowboy hat and standing close to the gate.

Keen blue eyes were looking over each passenger.

There was a wire-hard competence about the man which made him stand out from the crowd of people gathered to greet incoming passengers.

My eyes flickered to him and then were held there. The man pushed forward. "Donald Lam?" he asked. "Right," I told him.

Some of the strongest fingers I had ever encountered grasped my hand, squeezed it painfully, and then released it. A slow smile spread over the weather-beaten features. "I'm Kramer, K-R-A-M-E-R," he said, "from the Butte Valley Guest Ranch."

There had been about forty-five incoming passengers, yet this guy had unerringly picked me out.

"I presume you had a physical description," I said.

21

"Of you?"

"Yes."

"Hell no, they just told me to meet a guest, a Donald Lam, who is coming to stay for three weeks."

"Why did you pick me out of the crowd?" I asked.

He grinned and said, "Aw, I can nearly always pick them."

"How?"

"Well," he said, with a touch of Texas drawl, "I didn't pick you, you picked me."

"How come?"

"It's just a matter of psychology," he said. "I put on a cowboy hat, I stand out in front, I'm pretty well tanned from constant exposure to the weather.

"Guests who are coming to the ranch know that someone is going to be there to meet them and they're naturally wondering whether they'll have difficulty getting together, and whether transportation to the ranch will be furnished on schedule. So they look at me, start to look away, then do a double take and I can just see them saying to themselves, 'Now, I wonder if that's the man who is going to meet me.' "

Kramer grinned.

"That's good psychology," I said.

"You have to use psychology all the time on a guest ranch."

"You've studied psychology?" I asked.

"Hush," he said.

"What's wrong with that?"

"Everything. If a person knows you're using psychology on him, it makes it more difficult to get results."

"But *you* told *me*," I said.

"You're different," he said. "You said to me, 'Why did you pick me out of the crowd?' Most people say, 'I picked you out of the crowd right away, Mr. Kramer. As soon as I saw you, I knew who you were.'"

I let it go at that.

We went over and got my bags, took them out to a gaudy station wagon that had the picture of a butte with a trail winding around it, a long string of horsemen coming down the trail, and the words: "Butte Valley Guest Ranch" in big letters on the side. The tailgate had a picture of a bucking bronco, and over on the other side was a picture of a gay party on horseback, with a swimming pool and girls in skintight bathing suits.

"You must have an artist working at the ranch," I said.

"That art work pays off," Kramer told me. "Every time we go into town for supplies, I park the car, and you'll notice there's a container on the side of the door with a lot of folders telling about the ranch, rates and everything. You'd be surprised how much business we get from that.

"Tourists who are coming in to spend a few weeks in Tucson look at the artwork on the side of the car, pick up one of the folders, and the first thing anyone knows they're out at the ranch."

"More psychology?" I asked.

"More psychology."

"You run the place?"

"No, I work there."

"You must have a nickname," I said. "They don't call you 'Kramer,' do they?"

"No," he said with that grin, "they call me 'Buck.' "

"Short for your first name?"

"My first name," he said, "is Hobart. You can't imagine people calling me 'Hobe.' "

"Lots of dude wranglers use the nickname of 'Tex,' " I said.

He said, "This is Arizona."

"I seem to detect a little Texas accent," I told him.

"Well, don't mention it to anyone," he said, heaving my bags into the back of the car. "Come on, let's go."

We drove out of Tucson into the desert, out toward the mountains to the south and the east. It was a fairly long drive.

Buck Kramer talked about the desert, about the scenery, about the health-giving atmosphere, but he didn't talk any more about himself and he didn't talk much about the Butte Valley Guest Ranch.

We turned through a big gate that was open, ran a couple of miles up a fairly good slope, turned and came to a stop on a little mesa at the foot of the mountains that had now become a deep purple with the evening shadows.

Kramer parked the car, said, "I'll take your bags over to the cabin, and if you'll come with me I'll introduce you to Dolores Ferrol."

"Who's she?" I asked. "The manager?"

"The hostess," he said. "She welcomes everyone and tries to keep things moving— Here she is now."

Dolores Ferrol was a dish.

She was somewhere around twenty-six or twenty-seven, old enough to be adult, young enough to be luscious. She was dressed to show her curves and she had lots of curves to show, not big, bulgy curves but smooth, streamlined contours that would lodge in a man's thoughts and stay in his memory, to come disturbingly back from time to time, particularly at night.

Her large, dark eyes took me in, first with a little start of surprise and then with a cool appraisal.

She gave me her hand and let it stay in mine for a minute.

"Welcome to Butte Valley, Mr. Lam," she said. "I think you're going to like it here."

And when she said that she raised her eyes with just a flash of intimacy and gave my hand just the faintest suggestion of a squeeze.

"We've been expecting you. You're in Cabin number 3. We have cocktails in fifteen minutes, dinner in thirty-five minutes."

She turned to Kramer. "Buck, will you take his bags over?"

"Right away," Buck said.

"I'll show you your cabin," she said, and rested her hand gently on my arm.

We walked across a patio with a huge swimming

pool, tables, chairs and beach umbrellas. The patio was flanked by a row of cabins made to resemble log cabins.

Number 3 was second from the end, on the north side of the row.

Dolores held the door open.

I bowed and waited for her to enter first.

She came in, turned to me suddenly with swift intimacy. "Buck will be along with the bags in just a moment," she said. "We won't have a chance to discuss things now but I'll talk them over with you later. You know that you and I will be working together."

"I was told you would be in touch with me," I said.

"I sure will," she said.

Buck's high-heeled cowboy boots clomped along the cement as he tramped up on the porch with the bags.

"Here you are," he said. "See you later, Lam." He withdrew with suspicious promptness.

Dolores stood close to me. "It's going to be a pleasure to work with you, Mr. Lam," she said. "Donald—I'm Dolores."

"It will be *my* pleasure," I said. "How close shall we work?"

"Very close."

"How long," I asked, "have you been handling this job on the side?"

She was standing so close to me that I could feel the warmth of her body as she took her forefinger, placed the end of it against the tip of my nose, pushed gently, and said, "Now, don't be nosy, Donald." She laughed, showing parted red lips and pearly teeth.

I put my arm around her. She was so supple she seemed to melt into my arms; her lips came up to mine without the slightest hesitancy, a hot circle of passionate promise.

A moment later she pushed me back, using the very minimum of force and said, "Naughty, naughty, Donald. You must remember that you have a job to do and that I have a job to do. But when I fall for people I fall hard. You're nice—and I'm impulsive. Pardon the intimacy."

"*I* should beg *your* pardon," I said. "I was the aggressor."

"That's what *you* think," she said, and her laugh was throaty.

She reached in her pocket, produced facial tissue and solicitously wiped the lipstick from my face.

"You'll have to go and get your cocktail, Donald."

"I don't feel like a cocktail now," I said. "I'd rather stay here."

Her finger tips brushed against my hand. "So would I, but I'm the hostess, Donald. Come on."

She clutched my hand, pulled me gently to the door, said, "I'll introduce you around, but take it easy for a while because there's no one here you can use as bait right at the moment. However, we have a reservation for a Miss Doon who is due here tomorrow. She sounds interesting. She's a nurse. There's just a chance she might be what you want. Anyhow, you'll have a full two weeks and that's plenty of time to work."

"When is *he* coming?" I asked.

"He's due here tomorrow."

"You know all the details?" I asked.

Her laugh was seductive. "Donald," she said, "when I play a game I know all the cards."

"From the front or the back?" I asked.

She said, "A *good* player doesn't have to mark the cards.

"Now listen, Donald, there's one thing you have to help me on. If my employer ever got the idea I was keeping another job on the side, it would be just too bad. You're going to have to protect my secret on that."

"I don't do much talking," I told her.

She said, "It goes deeper than that. We're going to have to have conferences and in order to have those conferences take place without exciting too much suspicion, you're going to have to act the part."

"What part?"

"You're going to have to be tremendously infatuated with me, and while I'll appear to like you, I'll be conscious of the fact that my duties as hostess keep me from teaming up with any particular guy. I have to play the field and keep everybody happy.

"You'll sort of halfway resent that, be just a little mite jealous and be waiting for an opportunity to get me off to one side and alone whenever you have a chance. You think the thing over a little bit and look at it from my viewpoint. Then you'll see what I mean. I can't afford to let anyone think I'm holding down another job on the side."

"Who runs the place?" I asked.

"Shirley Gage," she said. "She's the widow of Leroy Willard Gage. She inherited the place and is making more money out of running it than she could by selling it, investing the money and collecting interest. Furthermore, she likes the life. She'll let the older ones— Well, any of the—"

"Go on and say it," I said.

"Well, I take care of the younger ones and act as hostess and see that everyone has a good time and gets together, but Shirley gives the older customers a little more of a play."

"Meaning she's lonely and looking for companionship?" I asked.

Dolores laughed and said, "Come on, here's where you turn in to get the cocktails. They usually limit the cocktails to about two to a customer. It depends on the customer and how he can take them. The cocktails aren't strong but they are free and they're not too bad. You can have either Manhattans or Martinis.

"Come on, Donald, in we go."

The room was well lighted with showcases containing Indian artifacts, paintings of the desert, Navajo rugs on the floor, a distinctive Western atmosphere.

There were some twenty people having cocktails, some of them in groups, some of them in twosomes.

Dolores clapped her hands and said, "Attention, everybody, here's our newest tenderfoot, Donald Lam of Los Angeles."

She took me by the hand and said, "Come on, Donald."

It was a remarkable performance. Some of these people she couldn't have known for more than twenty-four or forty-eight hours, but she was never at a loss for a name. She presented me to each person, went over to the bar with me, saw that I had a cocktail and then started mingling with the others.

It was quite evident that she was a great favorite with the guests, and she was an expert at the job of making them feel good. She'd join a group, enter into the conversation, then manage to leave without appearing to be breaking away, join some other group with a little pleasantry and always with a musical, sexy laugh.

Her dress was tight, her hips were smoothly streamlined and she used just exactly the right amount of slow, swaying motion as she walked. Nothing stiff or rigid; nothing exaggerated, but something about the motion that would arrest a man's attention.

Now and then some married man would break away from his wife to join the group where Dolores was talking. Whenever that happened, Dolores would find some excuse to leave within a matter of seconds, join some other group, or perhaps gravitate back to the group the man had left and chat naturally and animatedly with the wife.

People talked with me, they asked me about how long I intended to stay and they made guarded inquiries about my background. They weren't exactly personal to the point of being persistent but they had a mild curiosity.

For the most part, the people were between thirty-five and sixty. The men wore Pendletons, and here and there a face that was an angry red proclaimed a newcomer who had spent too much time in the sunlight.

The talk was largely about climate.

Some of the people came from the Middle West and talked about snowstorms; some of them came from the Coast and talked about smog and cloudiness.

I had my second cocktail, a bell rang and we filed in to dinner.

Dolores had a place for me at a table occupied by a broker from Kansas City, his wife, and a woman artist somewhere in her middle thirties.

We had a substantial dinner, prime ribs of beef, baked potatoes, onion rings, salad, dessert and hot rolls.

After dinner they started card games—bridge, gin rummy and poker. The poker game was a marathon affair, played for low stakes, where each player was trying to demonstrate his superiority.

It was a nice crowd.

Drinks could be ordered and charged on chits.

The artist who had been at the table with me monopolized my evening. She wanted to talk about colors, about creative art, about the menace of modern art, the deterioration of all types of artistic standards and the beauties of Western scenery.

She was lonely, widowed, wealthy and frustrated. She might have made good bait for a malingerer but her approach was too intellectual.

Motion pictures of the man with the whiplash injury diving off a springboard into a swimming pool in order to impress a young thing in a bathing suit would be valuable for a jury, but motion pictures of a guy sitting in a chair by the pool and discussing art with a woman wouldn't mean a damned thing.

I studied her carefully and decided Dolores was right in saying there was nothing presently available.

The artist's name was Faith Callison. She told me she did her sketching with a camera and colored films. She had a collection of slides which she would process into paintings later on in the winter in her studio, where she wouldn't be disturbed or distracted by other people.

"Ever sell your pictures as well as your paintings?" I asked.

She looked at me with sudden sharp interest. "Why do you ask that?"

Actually I had only been making conversation, but there was something in her manner which caused me to make a reappraisal of the situation.

"From what you said," I told her. "I gathered you took huge quantities of film. I like to take pictures myself, but the cost of the film is a factor *I* have to consider."

She gave a quick glance around the room, leaned closer to me, and said, "You know, Mr. Lam, that's the strangest thing that ever happened, having you put your finger on things that way. Actually I do sell my films— at times.

"You take last season, for instance. I had my eight-millimeter motion-picture camera with the zoom lens. I took pictures of people enjoying themselves and then afterwards I'd ask people if they wanted copies. Of course, I wasn't peddling films or anything like that. I made it appear that it was just a matter of accommodation from one shutterbug to another. But I did sell quite a bit of film."

"To people who didn't have their own cameras?" I asked.

"No," she said, "most of the sales were made to people who *did* bring their own cameras. In a place like this, a person who brings a motion-picture camera does so because of a desire to take home impressions of the place. He wants to show the folks back East what a real Western guest ranch looks like.

"Well, of course, if they're always taking pictures, they naturally can't appear in the pictures they take. So they love to get a few feet of film showing them against a colorful background."

"I see," I said thoughtfully. "I see that you've given quite a bit of thought to it."

She nodded.

"Any big sales?" I asked.

Again she looked at me curiously. "Well . . . yes.

There were two big sales. One was to an insurance company that wanted pictures of a certain man jumping off the diving board, and the other was one of the most peculiar orders I ever had. It was from a lawyer in Dallas. He wanted a copy of every foot of film I had taken on my vacation here on the ranch—just every single foot.

"That's why I'm here this year. I made enough out of that one sale to more than pay all my expenses this season."

"Well, my gosh, aren't *you* smart!" I said.

Then abruptly she changed the subject and went on to talk about art. I could see that she had become a little afraid she'd told me too much on too short acquaintance.

She told me she was taking up portrait painting and said I had an interesting face. She wanted to know something about my background. I told her I was a bachelor, that I had been too busy to get married, that I had had a long, hard day, excused myself and went to bed.

The silence of the desert was like a blanket. The clear, pure air was a benediction and I slept like a log.

Chapter 3

At seven-thirty the next morning a big iron triangle clanged out a summons. At seven-forty-five an Indian lad in a white coat brought orange juice. At eight o'clock there was coffee. Dolores knocked on my door.

"Good morning, Donald. How did you sleep?"

"Dead to the world," I told her.

"A breakfast ride leaves at eight-thirty, or you can have breakfast in the dining room at any time now."

"How far is the breakfast ride?"

"About twenty minutes," she said. "It will sharpen your appetite. The chuck wagon is already up there with a fire going and coffee ready. When the gang shows up, they'll scramble eggs and have bacon and toast, Dutch oven biscuits, broiled ham, sausages, anything you want."

"Rather hard on the horses, isn't it?" I asked.

"What?"

"Having guests put on so much weight."

She laughed. "The horses love it. They get to stand

35

around while the dudes—I mean the guests are feeding."

"Not dudes?" I asked.

"Heavens no," she said, "only among the help. Otherwise, they're invariably guests."

"I'm all ready to go," I said. "I'll take the breakfast ride."

"I thought you would."

I walked down to where the horses were being saddled. She walked beside me. A couple of times her hip brushed against mine. She gave me sidelong glances and said, "We're going to see a lot of each other during the season, Donald. This is a steady job, you know. After Helmann Bruno, there'll be others."

"Many others?"

"I think so. I think a whole procession."

"Perhaps I'll learn to ride."

Again she looked at me with a sidelong glance. "You might learn lots of things," she said. "It will be an opportunity for a liberal education."

We walked out to the horses. Buck Kramer sized me up. "What kind of a horse do you want, Donald?"

"Anything you have left over," I told him.

"You want a spirited one?"

"Fix up the other guests," I said. "I'll take anything that's left over."

"We have all kinds."

"Suit yourself."

"There's a bay over there that's all saddled. Get on and try the stirrups."

I swung into the saddle and put weight on the balls of my feet, shifted my position from right to left, back left to right, then sat in the middle of the horse. I put gentle neck pressure on the reins, swung the horse to the left, then to the right and got off. "Perfectly all right," I said. "Those stirrups fit me swell."

"The stirrups fit you but the horse doesn't," Kramer said.

"What's the matter?"

"You're entitled to a better horse."

He nodded his head to a stableboy, held up one finger, and in a minute the boy came out leading a horse that was walking on eggs.

Kramer threw the saddle and bridle on him, said, "You'll take him, Lam. . . . Where did you learn to ride?"

"I don't ride," I said. "I just sit in the saddle."

"The hell you don't," he said. "You're tall in the saddle. This horse is inclined to shy a little bit. He doesn't do it because he's really afraid, he just does it to be sociable and give his rider a thrill. Pick him up when he does it but not too much."

"Okay," I said.

Dudes came straggling in and most of them were helped into the saddle. At eight-thirty, we took off.

We were riding along a jeep road, but there were marks of horses in the center and wagon wheels on the side. We went up a canyon, out of the sunlight into the shadows. Buck, in the lead, put his horse in a slow canter.

The dudes bounced around behind, some of them trying to grip the barrel of the horse with their knees and heels, others hanging on to the saddle horn, others just bouncing. Very few of them sat relaxed in the saddle.

Buck looked back a couple of times and I saw him watching me carefully.

My horse was light on his feet. You could sit in the middle of him and it was like being in a rocking chair.

We jogged along for ten or fifteen minutes, winding along the banks of a dry arroyo, then came to a sage-covered flat. There were hitching racks around the edges of the flat and, in the center, a buckboard was drawn up with the tailgate down, a rather elderly, grizzled Mexican with a cook's hat and a white coat presiding over a bed of coals and a barbecue grate. There were dozens of frying pans and three or four young Mexican boys acting as helpers.

The dudes swung out of their saddles with various groans and heaves and walked stiff-legged over to the barbecue grate, stood around interfering with the cook, holding their hands out to the warmth of the coals, then moving over to a big picnic table and benches on the other side of the buckboard.

They drank coffee out of enameled mugs; ate eggs, bacon, sausage and ham out of enamelware plates; had biscuits and honey, brown toast, lots of marmalade and jelly. Then they sat around smoking cigarettes and relaxing until the sun came over the ridge and flooded the flat with brilliant sunlight.

Buck called for riders on the upper trail and about half of the crowd elected to go back to the ranch; the other half swung on the upper trail.

I took the upper trail with Kramer.

"You sit that horse pretty good," he said. "You've got a nice hand. He has a tender mouth."

"I like horses."

"That's nothing," he said, "horses like you. . . . How did you happen to come here?"

I said, "Somebody told me about it, a friend of mine."

"Who was it?" Buck asked. "I remember virtually everybody who is here."

"Fellow by the name of Smith," I said. "I didn't know him too well, met him in a bar one night. He was just back from here, had quite a sunburn, and told me about the wonderful times he'd had here."

"I see," Kramer said, and didn't say anything more.

The upper trail was one that went up out of the canyon, around a high mesa, forked to the left, came out on a point where we could look down over the desert to the south and west, along the mountains to the north; then the trail went down a steep incline which brought a lot of squeals from the women, and occasionally a masculine voice would boom out, "Whoa, now! Whoa! Take it easy, boy! Whoa!"

Kramer turned in the saddle to look at me and winked.

I gave the horse his head and he picked his sure-footed way on down the steep trail, down to the bottom of the canyon through sagebrush, and about eleven o'clock we came to the ranch house.

We unsaddled and went out to the swimming pool. They served coffee.

Most of the guests went swimming.

Dolores showed up in an elastic bathing suit that clung to her like the skin to a sausage.

"Coming in, Donald?" she asked.

"Perhaps later."

She leaned over, dipped her hand into the water, held up slim fingers, snapped them at me, throwing a tantalizing spray of drops in my face. "Come on in now," she said, and ran down the ramp as lightly as a deer.

I went into my cabin, put on a bathing suit, came out and jumped in the water.

Dolores was over at the other end of the pool but, after a moment, she came over to me.

"You aren't big, but you're certainly well built, Donald," she said, her right hand rested lightly on my bare shoulder.

"Talk about being built," I said, looking her over.

"Yes?" she asked, and the fingers of her right hand left a trail of fire down my bare back; then she was swimming away and talking to a bulging woman in her fifties who was splashing around in the pool; then she was over batting her eyelashes at one of the men and, almost immediately, swam over to his wife and spent a few minutes with her.

I did a couple of dives from the springboard, went

out on one of the fiber mats and let the sun soak into my skin, then I went in, took a shower, came out and sat at one of the tables.

Dolores came over and said, "Melita Doon will be here for lunch. She came in on the morning plane. Buck's gone to pick her up."

"Know anything about her?" I asked.

"Only that she's a nurse, in her late twenties. She should be okay."

A man's voice said, "Hey, Dolores, show my wife how to do that backstroke, will you?"

"I certainly will," she said and leaned intimately forward to hold my eyes for a minute. "See you later, Donald," she said, and was gone.

After that, she was a perfect swimming instructor, then she supervised exercises with some of the women who wanted to take off a few pounds where it counted, and then the guests straggled away to the showers to get ready for lunch.

Melita Doon arrived about twelve-thirty. Dolores Ferrol went out to meet her while Buck Kramer took her things into her cabin. She had Cabin number 2, right next to mine.

As they walked past where I was sitting, Dolores gave me a purposeful glance, then looked back to Melita Doon and let her eyes run up and down Melita's figure, the way one woman will when she's sizing up another.

Melita was a blonde, about twenty-six or -seven, not over five feet two or three, and perfectly proportioned.

There wasn't an ounce of weight on her that didn't belong, but she had all the things that did belong, although on a small scale. She walked with an easy grace, her legs slender and aristocratic.

The thing that caught my eye was *her* eyes.

She flashed me one swift look then glanced away, but I could see that her eyes were hazel and uneasy. She looked frightened.

Then the girls went on past me toward the cabin.

Dolores knew that I would be watching them from the rear and exaggerated the swing of her hips just slightly so that I'd know she knew I was watching.

They were still in Cabin number 2 when the luncheon bell rang.

Lunch was out by the pool. It was fruit salad, consomme, with hot biscuit and chipped beef in creamed gravy.

Buck Kramer sauntered over while I was eating. "All alone?" he asked.

I nodded.

Kramer sank into the chair on the opposite side of the table.

This wasn't what I had in mind. I was hoping that Dolores would bring Melita out and we'd have a chance to get acquainted, but there was no way I could turn Buck down without being rude to him.

"Lunch?" I asked.

"Not this stuff," Buck said, waving his hand in an inclusive gesture. "I eat in the kitchen. I like a little more meat and a little less fruit. How did you like that horse?"

"Fine."

"He's a nice horse. We don't let everybody ride him."

"Thanks."

"Don't thank me. He needs the exercise; but you know how it is, you let a good horse out to a poor rider and in no time at all the rider is just as bad as he ever was and the horse is just as bad as the rider.

"People don't realize it, but horses are very sensitive to a rider. They know people. The minute you put your foot in a stirrup and pick up the reins, the horse knows just about all you know about riding. By the time you've settled yourself in the saddle and given him the first turn signal, he can tell all about you, whether you take your coffee black or with cream and sugar."

Kramer grinned.

"You seem to be a pretty good judge of riders," I said.

"You have to be in this business. . . . Take the guy that comes out with a new pair of cowboy boots, a tailor-made Pendleton outfit, a five-gallon hat and a silk scarf around his neck. He swaggers over and says he'd like to have a horse that is a little better than the average dude horse. He hates to be at the tail end of the procession.

"You look the guy over and if he's wearing spurs the first thing you do is to tell him that it's one of the regulations of the ranch that guests can't wear spurs. Then you watch how he takes the spurs off, and by that time you know enough about him to give him one of the oldest, safest plugs on the place.

"That day he'll give you a ten-dollar tip and tell you he'd like a better horse for the next day. He has a girl friend that he wants to impress. He tells you about the riding he's done in Montana, Idaho, Wyoming and Texas."

"What do you do?" I asked.

"Take the ten bucks and give him another plug the next day. If you gave the guy a real horse, he'd have a runaway and wind up either falling off or getting bucked off."

"Doesn't he resent getting a plug after he's given you ten bucks?"

"In a way," Kramer said, "but you have a line that goes with it. You tell him he'll have to be alert; that that horse is usually very demure, but if he could take advantage of a rider he would. You say that he spilled a couple of people last year and since that time you've never dared to put anyone on him except an expert rider.

"The guy goes and tells his girl all about that, gives you ten bucks more, and tells you it's a good horse and he wants to have him all the time he's here."

Kramer yawned.

Dolores came out of Cabin number 2, stood in the door waiting, caught my eye, saw Buck sitting there and went back into the cabin.

"You've eaten already?" I asked Buck.

"No, I'm going to eat now."

He scraped back his chair, looked down at me and said, "You know, Lam, if you don't mind my saying so, there's something a little peculiar about you."

"How come?"

He said, "You're not talking."

"Am I supposed to talk?"

"Hell," he said, "people come out here and spill their guts, particularly the people who can ride. They tell me about the dude ranches they've been at, the camping trips they've been on, the hours they've spent in the saddle. . . . Where the hell did you learn to ride?"

"I don't ride," I said. "I just sit on the horse."

He snorted and walked away.

No sooner had he left than Dolores came out of the cabin bringing Melita Doon with her. They walked over toward the main house, then abruptly Dolores swung over my way and said, "Miss Doon, let me present my friend, Donald Lam."

I rose and bowed. "Pleased to meet you," I said.

Hazel eyes surveyed me with a frankness that I found embarrassing.

"Hello," she said, and gave me her hand.

It was a cool hand with slender but strong fingers.

She had changed to riding clothes now, a tailored outfit that showed her slender figure to advantage.

"It's just at the lunch hour," Dolores said to Melita Doon, "and I'm famished. . . . Look, Donald, why don't we sit here with you? You seem to be all alone."

"That," I said, "would be wonderful."

Dolores caught the eye of one of the waiters and beckoned him. I drew up some chairs for the two girls. They seated themselves.

Dolores said, "Donald and I are buddies. . . . He's nice."

Melita smiled at me.

A waiter came and took orders.

Melita studied me with a certain frank curiosity that was far from the casual scrutiny a girl on vacation would give a stranger.

I had a sudden flash of panic as I wondered if Dolores had been a little too obvious in plugging me to Melita. Dolores was a girl who didn't waste time, and Melita was a girl who didn't overlook the obvious—and there were times when Dolores could be pretty darned obvious.

We were halfway through the meal when Buck Kramer came over with a telephone message for Dolores. "Helmann Bruno is going to be in on the three-thirty plane," he said.

"Well, that's fine," Dolores said. "Will you meet him, Buck?"

"I'll meet him," Buck said.

I was watching Melita's face when Buck gave Dolores the message. I could have sworn that there was a sudden flash of sheer panic in her eyes, then she lowered her eyes demurely to her plate and managed to toy with the coffee cup until she either had herself under control or until my imagination had quit playing tricks on me.

"Another guest?" she asked, raising her eyes to Dolores.

"Another guest," Dolores said cheerfully. "They come and go all the time."

"Bruno," Melita said, "that's an unusual name. Helmann Bruno—the name sort of rings a bell someway. Is he an author? Did he write a book or something?"

"No," Dolores said, "he's some sort of a prize winner. He won a contest which entitles him to two weeks' stay at the guest ranch here. I imagine he must have something on the ball or he wouldn't have won a contest over a whole flock of contestants."

"Perhaps that's where I've heard the name," Melita said, "in connection with winning some sort of a contest. It must have been advertised in the magazines or something."

Dolores was elaborately casual. "I wouldn't know," she said. "I just try to keep people happy here and don't pry into their backgrounds."

She emphasized, subtly, the words "don't pry into their backgrounds."

Melita flashed her a quick glance, then again looked down at her coffee.

Dolores looked at me. There was a puzzled look in her eyes.

We finished the meal, and Dolores said, "Well, this is the time of the siesta. Everybody relaxes for a while after lunch, then we have some golf games in the afternoon, some more swimming, and we have a nice tennis court and some tennis matches. Do you like tennis, Melita?"

"No," she said, "I like to swim and I love horseback riding, but aside from that I'm pretty awkward when it comes to athletics."

I let it go at that and went to my cabin, ostensibly to take a siesta.

Chapter 4

I made it a point that afternoon to be sitting out by the pool where I could see the Butte Valley Guest Ranch station wagon when it drove up. I wanted an opportunity to size up Helmann Bruno as he got out of the machine, because it frequently happens that a malingerer will give himself away by some little involuntary action before he realizes people are watching.

I saw a swirl of dust down the road, then the station wagon emerged with Buck Kramer at the wheel. The car made a wide turn and came into the parking lot reserved for incoming guests.

The man who shared the front seat with Kramer sat very still.

Kramer got out, ran around the car and opened the door.

Bruno thrust out a cautious leg, then another leg, then a cane.

Kramer took one of Bruno's hands and eased him out of the car.

Bruno stood, stiff-legged, swaying slightly, then with

the cane in one hand and the other on Kramer's arm he came slowly forward toward the swimming pool.

Kramer said, as he passed me, "This is one of the guests now, Mr. Bruno. This is Mr. Lam."

Bruno, tall, stiff-waisted, with large, dark eyes, shifted his gaze to me, smiled, put the cane in his left hand, extended his right hand, said, "How do you do, Mr. Lam."

"Mr. Bruno," I said. "Pleased to meet you."

"I'm sorry to be so clumsy," he said. "I was in an automobile accident and it left me pretty unsteady on my pins."

"Bones broken?" I asked.

He disengaged his hand from mine and rubbed the back of his neck. "A whiplash," he said. "At least that's what the doctors tell me it is. It's damned annoying. I've had these headaches and dizzy spells. . . . I came here to take a good, long rest. I think just sitting out in the sunlight will do me good."

He moved his right hand over to take hold of the head of the cane.

I noticed the ring on his right hand. A huge gold affair with a ruby in the center, the gold twisted so that it looked like a knotted rope, with the ruby in the center of the big flat knot.

"Just step this way, please, Mr. Bruno," Kramer said. "We'll register, and then I'll show you your cabin. I believe you're to have Cabin number 12. Take it easy, now."

"It's all right," Bruno said, apologetically. "I'm just

taking it a little slow, that's all. These dizzy spells, they hit me occasionally."

With Kramer supporting him they moved off toward the registration desk.

Dolores Ferrol had been hurrying toward us from the other end of the patio. She didn't get there before Bruno and Kramer started off, but she was near enough to get the picture.

She came swinging up to me. "Get a load of that," she said. "We're licked. We'll never trap that guy."

I said, "Perhaps he's smelled a rat. One thing's certain—we've drawn a blank so far."

She stood looking after them and there was a look of frustration in her eyes, then she said, somewhat defiantly, "Let me get him out in the moonlight, start a little seductive stuff and he'll come to life in a big way."

"Not in front of a motion-picture camera," I said. "You need daylight for motion pictures."

We sauntered over toward the registration desk. When Bruno and Kramer came out, Kramer introduced him to Dolores.

Dolores batted her eyelashes at him and let him look at the low-cut V of her blouse. "Rheumatism, Mr. Bruno?" she asked. "This is the greatest place in the world to clear up rheumatic pains."

"Automobile accident," he explained with tired patience. "A whiplash injury. I thought this would be the place for it, but I guess I made a mistake getting so far from my doctor. However, I'm getting all this for nothing. I won a two-week trip here in a contest."

"You did!" Dolores exclaimed, looking at him with admiration in her eyes. "*I've* always wanted to win one of those contests but I finally quit trying. I just don't have the brains."

"This one was dead easy," Bruno said, and turned to Kramer. "You'll take my baggage over?"

"I'll take you over, and you can lie down," Kramer said. "Then I'll bring your baggage over. After that I'll go back and see if I can locate that bag that you're missing. The plane company seemed to feel sure it would be in on the next plane, and that should be in by the time I get there."

"Confounded nuisance," Bruno said. "They have the latest engineering on airplanes. They put them on drawing boards, test them in wind tunnels, give you the deluxe service once you get aboard. But when it comes to handling passengers and baggage on the ground they treat you like human cattle and try to use the methods that were in existence when the Ford trimotor was the flagship of the fleet."

Kramer laughed. "On the other hand, it's certainly surprising they do as well as they do. People are traveling in droves and hordes these days."

Bruno's voice had the querulous note of the chronic invalid. "I have troubles," he said. "I guess I see the negative side."

He bowed stiffly to Dolores, said, "I'll see you again," and then he and Kramer moved over toward the cabin at the other end of the string.

"I've never run into one like this before," Dolores said.

"The guy's clever," I told her. "Or else he's really hurt."

When Kramer came·out, I said, "If you're going into town after that bag that was lost, I'd like to ride in with you. I have some things I want to buy."

"I'll get them for you," Kramer said.

"No," I told him, "I'd like to pick them out myself. If you don't have anyone coming back with you, I can—"

"Heck," he said, "this station wagon runs back and forth all the time. That's what it's for, the convenience of guests. In the morning when I'm out riding with the guests, one of the other employees takes it in. But in the afternoon I make four and five trips a day at times. Come on, get in."

I climbed in the front seat of the station wagon beside him.

"Imagine a guy like that coming to a guest ranch," Kramer said, as he started the car. "You'd think he'd go to a sanitarium."

"Of course," I said, "he won a two-weeks stay here as a result of some contest or other."

"We get them every once in a while," Kramer said. "Guys that come here because they won a contest. It's some baking powder company, I think, that has a series of prizes for people who can write the best fifty-word article on why this baking powder is the best. I've never run onto the ads, myself, but we've had several people here who filled out the entrance blanks and won this particular prize. I understand some of the prizes include a trip to Honolulu."

"Well," I said, reassuringly, "two weeks here will do this fellow a lot of good."

"There's one thing certain," Kramer said, "he won't be riding any horses. I won't have to listen to him telling me about how he rode when he was a boy and how he once had a spirited horse that was a little more than the ordinary person could handle, then bribe me to get a little better horse the next ride. I get so fed up with that stuff. Every one of them gets as good a horse as he can ride.

"If I'd let those guys ride the kind of horses they would select for themselves, we'd have dudes digging postholes with their heads all over the trails. Oh, well, I guess we all have our problems."

I grinned at him reassuringly.

"How did you like that horse *you* had this morning?" he asked.

"Fine," I said.

"You got along with him all right," Kramer said. "Some fellows have too heavy a hand and the horse resents them. He starts fighting the bit and the reins and then he begins to fight the rider, so they hold him in even more, and that's bad."

"Pile them off?" I asked.

"Heavens no, nothing like that. We won't let a horse on the ranch that bucks off a rider, but the horse gets restive and nervous and comes back soaking wet with sweat. The rider has been fighting the horse and he's all sweaty and hasn't had a good time.

"You'd be surprised how animals understand these things. These horses know that they make their living by taking dudes out over trails and while they sometimes resent a rider, for the most part they have a very definite sense of responsibility. We've never had one yet that would spill a dude on the trail."

"Must be quite a responsibility, getting horses of that sort and keeping them in training, and properly exercised," I said.

Kramer grinned. "Say, how did we get to talking about *my* troubles? Why don't we talk about yours?"

"I don't have any," I told him.

We rode into the airport, just getting acquainted and talking around in circles. Kramer didn't loosen up on anything except generalities. The minute I'd mention the name of some particular guest, Kramer would dry up like a clam, then change the subject. I got the idea that it was a matter of policy never to discuss one guest with another guest.

We got to the airport and I called Bertha Cool from a telephone booth.

"Donald," she said, "how are you coming?"

"Everything okay so far," I said, "except the job is going to blow up."

"What do you mean?"

I said, "This guy, Bruno, is either really injured or he's too clever to fall for anything as crude as the trap that's been set for him."

"You mean you can't cut the mustard?" Bertha asked accusingly.

"It isn't a question of whether I can cut the mustard," I said, "it's a question of whether there's any mustard there to be cut. The guy probably really has had a whiplash injury. I'm going to call Breckinridge, but I thought I'd give you a ring first and let you know what's in the wind."

"My God," Bertha said, "he can't back out on the deal now. You're there for three weeks with all expenses paid and we're collecting sixty dollars a day straight through."

"I'm not going to hold him to it," I said. "I think when he hears my report, he'll want to change his tactics and recall me."

"Recall you!" Bertha screamed into the telephone. "Why that so-and-so can't back out on a bargain like that."

"Let's not let him feel we're that hungry for business," I said. "We have other things we can do."

"You let me call him," Bertha said. "I'll talk with him."

"No," I told her, "I've got to make a report personally. I'm just letting you know. I'll be in touch with you."

I hung up while she was still arguing, and put through a call to Breckinridge. I was in luck. As soon as I gave my name to his secretary, he came on the phone at once.

"Hello, Lam," he said, "you're out there in Tucson?"

"That's right."

"How's the dude ranch?"

"Fine."

"Getting along with Dolores all right?"

"Splendid!"

"That's good," he said, and then after a moment, "What seems to be on your mind?"

I said, "This fellow Bruno isn't going to be a pushover."

"No? How come?"

I said, "The fellow isn't sailing under any false colors. He arrived by plane this afternoon and told everyone he was there at the ranch because he'd won a contest, that he'd been seriously injured in an automobile accident, that he had a whiplash injury and he was going to have to keep very, very quiet.

"He's walking around with a cane, and his hand on the arm of the wrangler who handles the horses."

"The hell he is!" Breckinridge exclaimed.

"That's right."

Breckinridge thought that over, then gave a low whistle. "All right, Donald," he said, "come on back."

"Just like that?" I asked.

"Just like that," he said. "We're going to pay the guy off."

"I'm just reporting progress," I said. "After all, he may still be faking. It may be we can catch him off first base."

"I don't think we'd better try it," Breckinridge said. "I'm glad you called me, Donald. We'd better pay off. If he's on the up-and-up, those whiplash injuries can really run into money. Just grab a plane and come home."

I said, "Don't be in quite such a hurry. Give me another day on the job. I want to size this situation up. I'm just reporting progress because I thought you'd like to know."

"Splendid, Lam," he said. "That's splendid. I'm glad you did. Now, don't get me wrong, Lam, this isn't going to make any difference as far as you're concerned. We'll adjust with the agency, all right, on a basis of three weeks' work, but I just don't believe in taking chances with a genuine whiplash injury, not if we can get any decent kind of settlement."

"You can hold off for a day, all right?" I asked.

"Well," he said, paused for a moment, then added, "yes, we can hold off for a day all right."

I said, "I had a chance to ride into town, so I thought I'd give you a ring and let you know what's cooking."

"Lam," he said, "I'm available all the time. I make it a rule to be where I can be reached whenever anything important comes up. You just give your name to my secretary and she'll see that a call goes through to me. Now, you call me tomorrow and let me know, will you?"

"Okay."

"Be *sure* to call."

"I surely will," I told him, and hung up.

I went out into the airport and picked up Kramer. He was hanging around the soda counter having a chocolate malt. The piece of baggage showed up on schedule and we went back to the ranch.

I had cocktails, dinner and afterwards there was dancing.

I danced with Dolores.

She had a very intimate, seductive way of dancing without appearing to be too close.

"Been making any passes at Bruno?" I asked.

She said, "The man's an iceberg. He's *really* injured, Donald. This is a new angle. I never expected to encounter one like this.

"They told me they wouldn't send anyone out here unless they were sure he was faking. I don't know how they could have felt sure about this fellow."

"Perhaps they aren't," I said. "They may have taken a chance and got the wrong answer."

"Are *you* going to be around, Donald?"

"I don't know. Why?"

"I'd hate to have you go back just when we're getting acquainted."

I said, "Anyone would think I was the one who was malingering the way you're putting it up to me."

Her eyes came up to mine. "I'm putting it up to you, as you expressed it, because I like you," she said.

The music ended at that moment, and Dolores emphasized her remarks by pressing her hips close to mine for just the fraction of a second and making a little twisting motion. Then she was smiling up into my face and one of the other guests was bearing down on her for a dance.

"How do you keep from antagonizing all the wives?" I asked.

"It's an art," she told me, and turned to the approaching guest with a smile that was completely impersonal.

I watched the next dance. She was properly demure, smiling from time to time at her partner, then letting her eyes look over the other guests, sizing them up, making certain they were having a good time.

Any married woman would have caught that look and appreciated it. It showed Dolores was doing her duty.

I couldn't be sure about Bruno, but there was one thing I could say for certain, Dolores was a remarkably clever young woman.

Activities at the guest ranch were timed so that guests could retire at an early hour.

On two nights a week they had dancing, but the dancing was limited to an hour, then the music was turned off and the guests were encouraged to get into bed early.

On two nights a week they had a campfire out in a second patio where they had chairs in a circle around the campfire. Mesquite logs gave forth flames and then burned down to coals. Cowboy entertainers played guitars and sang Western songs. These entertainers were usually a group who went from ranch to ranch entertaining the various guests.

Then occasionally they would have group evenings where two or three of the guest ranches would get together for a joint entertainment. These entertainments would be more elaborate, would include both dancing and campfire gatherings with cowboy singing.

The idea was to have enough variety so that the guests were kept entertained but to see that they got plenty of sleep.

I retired to my cabin early because Melita Doon had pleaded a headache and turned in, and Helmann Bruno had utilized his injuries as an excuse to be taken down to his cabin.

Someone had dug up a wheelchair for him and he was taking to this wheelchair like a duck to water.

Dolores Ferrol was frustrated but concealing her frustration amid the myriad activities of a good hostess on a social night. She was determined to get Bruno to open up.

She saw that everyone met everyone else, saw that the groups were shifted from time to time so that the guests didn't get into groups that would in time develop into partisan cliques.

In short, Dolores was thoroughly competent and was doing a great job, but she wanted very much to talk with me, and I could see that after the formal entertainment broke up she intended to discuss the case in great detail.

As far as I was concerned, there was no case to discuss—not yet, anyway, and before I became involved with Dolores I wanted to be definitely certain about Melita Doon. There was something about that girl that bothered me.

I started toward the cabin, yawning ostentatiously.

Dolores was at my side almost instantly.

"You're leaving, Donald?"

"It's been a hard day."

She laughed. "Don't kid me, you're one of these wiry guys who could take a dozen days like that—or are you afraid of the night?"

I shifted the subject back to business. "What about Melita Doon?" I said. "She isn't the usual type who's looking for adventure and romance. She isn't a girl who's nuts about horses and wants to ride, nor is she a shutterbug who wants to come out in the desert to get a collection of colored pictures.

"Why is she here?"

"I'll be darned if I know," Dolores said. "I've seen them all, all the different types, but this girl has me stopped.

"You've classified the three types who come here, all right. When they're on the make, they're very much on the make. The first people they meet are the cowpunchers and these gals literally throw themselves at the wranglers. The wranglers get so terribly bored with it that a woman can virtually peel off her clothes, and they'll yawn, turn their backs and go to saddling the horses.

"Then there's the horsey type. The wranglers get along fine with those if they don't think they know more than they do. If they genuinely love the horses and love to ride, we see that they get good mounts and have a good time.

"Then, of course, there are the shutterbugs, the artists and the people who love the solitude and vast spaces of the desert. They can't get out by themselves, but this is the next thing to it. They come here and they keep to themselves."

"Well," I said, "Melita Doon came here and she's keeping to herself. How about the latter type? Do you think she's one who loves the solitude and takes this because it's the nearest approach to it?"

Dolores shook her head. "Not that girl. There's something on her mind. She's here for— Somehow, Donald, I feel she's here for a purpose."

"I get the same impression," I said.

"Well," she said, "she's in the cabin next to you and this is the third time you've yawned prodigiously in the past fifteen minutes. I thought perhaps the expectation of . . . well . . ."

She smiled enticingly.

I said, "Somebody must have doped the coffee. I'm dead on my feet. See you tomorrow, Dolores."

"Tomorrow?" she asked.

I faced her. "This is a pretty good job you have here, Dolores."

"I make it a good job."

"Does it pay well?"

"I make it pay well," she said. "I know what I'm doing, I'm doing a darned good job. Because of me the guests leave with a lot better impression of the place than they would if I weren't here. I charge money for that, and I get money for it."

"And," I said, "no one knows about this other job

that you're holding down, the one for the insurance company?"

Her eyes suddenly became quizzical. "What are you doing, Donald, leading up to a species of blackmail?"

"I just don't like to be in the dark," I said.

"You can have lots of fun in the dark. . . . Go on," she said, "what are you getting at?"

"How did you get this second job?" I asked.

"That was an idea that the Claims Department had."

"Homer Breckinridge?"

"If you want to know, yes."

"Then he's been here at the ranch?"

"Yes."

"When was he here?"

"Last year."

"And he saw you working and got the idea for this setup, having people come down here ostensibly as contest winners?"

"Yes."

"How many have you had?"

"I don't think Mr. Breckinridge would like to have me tell you that."

"Look, Dolores," I told her, "we're both of us working for Breckinridge. Now, this conversation is designed to keep relations harmonious and happy."

"You're afraid you might be poaching on Breckinridge's preserves?"

"That's one of the things I have in mind."

She thought that over.

"I'd hate to do anything that would jeopardize our jobs," I said. "They're good jobs for both of us. Breckinridge isn't a fool. He sent me down here on an experimental run, so to speak. . . . Now, you've had other people before in my place. What happened to them?"

"I don't know," she said. "They didn't come back. It was a one-time proposition."

"Exactly," I told her. "I don't want to be a one-time proposition. I'll see you tomorrow, Dolores?"

She stood hesitant for a moment, then said softly, "Good night, Donald," and walked away.

Melita Doon's cabin was already dark. She had turned in half an hour ago. Evidently she didn't waste much time getting into bed. She wasn't the sort who would have a long ritual of beauty treatment before turning out the light.

I took a good long look around my cabin, exploring it. There was a porch, a little sitting room, a bedroom and a bath, a large closet, a vented gas heater and a small back porch.

The architecture suggested that during the fall and winter there were cold mornings and evenings, and that at one time there had been two wood heating stoves—one in the little sitting room and one in the bedroom. That small back porch had been built to hold a supply of firewood. Then, with the advent of gas, vented radiant heaters had been put in and there was no longer any need for the back porch or the wood box.

The distance between my cabin and the one occupied

by Melita Doon was about ten feet. Her bedroom window was opposite mine, but staggered in such a way that I couldn't see into it except for a corner of the bedroom.

Melita was evidently not only in bed but was something of a fresh-air fiend, because the window was open, and the lace curtains had been looped to the side so there would be a circulation of the fresh desert air.

I undressed, showered, got into pajamas, crawled into bed and went to sleep.

I don't know exactly how much time had elapsed when I awoke with a start. Some noise, or something, had awakened me.

A bright light was shining into one corner of my bedroom.

I jumped out of bed and had started for the bedroom door, before I realized that the source of the light was coming catercorner from Melita Doon's bedroom window.

By standing close against my window, I could look into the corner of her bedroom.

I saw a shadow moving, then another shadow. Very definitely there were two shadows.

I heard the voice of a man, a low-pitched insistent rumble. I heard a woman's voice say something, short and fast. Then the man's voice again. This time in a peremptory order.

Suddenly Melita Doon came into the corner of the bedroom and into my line of vision.

She was wearing a thin nightie with some sort of a

filmy, fluffy robe thrown over it that was apparently sheer to the point of being diaphanous.

A man's hand reached out and clamped around her wrist.

I couldn't see the man. All I could see was the hand, but I saw a ring. It was a heavy gold ring. There was a ruby in the center. I saw the red fire of it.

I couldn't swear to it in the brief glimpse I had, but it looked a lot like the ring that had been worn earlier that evening by Helmann Bruno.

The Doon cabin was suddenly dark. The lights had been on for not more than two minutes after I awakened.

I gently raised my window but could hear no sound of voices. I tiptoed to the front door and left it open so that if Bruno left the place I would be able to see him and see how he was walking, whether rapidly and with a normal gait or whether he was still groping his way along with a cane.

After some ten minutes when he didn't come out, I tiptoed out to my back door, stepped on the porch and looked over at the adjoining cottage.

There was a back door there that was exactly the same as the one on my cabin, and the porch arrangement was the same. It would have been readily possible for him to have left that cabin by the back door, then turned to the right instead of the left so that he would have circled away from my cabin and been concealed until after he had moved over to the service road.

The service road was unpaved. It was simply a dirt road that they used in delivering furniture or provisions to the different cabins. It wasn't particularly dusty because the soil had a lot of decomposed granite in it, but it didn't have a hard surface.

I dressed, slipped a small flashlight in my pocket and eased out of the back door of my cabin. I surreptitiously worked my way through the shadows until I came to the service road, then I took off my coat, used it to shield the beam of my flashlight, and checked the road for tracks.

Sure enough there were the tracks of a man's shoes going down the road in the direction of the Bruno cabin.

I didn't dare follow them all the way but I did follow them far enough to see that the man was taking good, healthy, normal strides.

There was one thing I couldn't control and that was my own tracks. In a road of that sort, everything that moves leaves a track, and a skilled tracker can detect those thin indentations and follow them.

I could, of course, have eliminated my tracks by brushing my palms over them and smoothing the dirt, but that would have attracted even more attention than the tracks themselves.

Cowpunchers have to track saddle and pack horses in the morning in order to find out where the stock has strayed during the night. They have to track cattle. They not only become expert at reading tracks but at noticing anything that is out of the ordinary.

I turned around and walked back along the dirt road, making no effort to conceal my tracks. I doubted very much that Bruno would know someone had tried to track him but I knew that the first cowpuncher who rode down that road on horseback would notice the tracks. If he came along in a jeep or a pickup, he wouldn't be so apt to pick them up. I'd probably be suspected of philandering. I had to take that chance.

I worked my way cautiously around the cabins, through the shadows, back to my own cabin and went to bed.

Chapter 5

Kramer had told me that they fed the horses around six o'clock, started saddling up at a little after seven, grooming the horses and getting them ready for the morning ride which started around eight-thirty on normal days. On the two or three mornings a week when they had breakfast rides, the rides started earlier.

There was no breakfast ride scheduled, so I was up and down at the stables a little after six-thirty.

About six-forty-five the wranglers came out from the dining room where they had been having their breakfast.

Kramer looked at me in surprise. "What in the world are you doing?" he asked.

"The curse of a nervous disposition," I told him. "No matter what time I go to bed at night I wake at daylight, and after I wake up I want to get up and get into action.

"If I'm in the city, I can sometimes control the impulse but out here where the air is pure, it seems positively wasteful to spend daylight hours in bed."

He grinned and said, "I guess you're right. I don't know. I've never been able to find out. I'd like to try it sometime.

"Look, Lam, you're a good enough rider so you can go out by yourself. If you want, I'll throw a saddle on your horse and you can take him out and give him a little exercise."

"What time does the ride start?" I asked.

"This morning the ride starts around nine o'clock. You'll go crazy trying to find something to do between now and then."

"What do you do now? Feed the horses?"

"No, we groom them and saddle them, but I'm going to town. I've got to take Mr. and Mrs. Wilcox in to the nine o'clock plane. They want to be in there by eight-thirty and they preferred to have breakfast at the airport. They're just getting a cup of coffee here."

"Fine," I told him. "I'll ride in with you. That'll give me something to do."

Kramer laughed and said, "You're the exact opposite of most of the guests we have here. Most of them like to come straggling in for breakfast and then hold up the string on the morning rides. . . . Okay, we'll be leaving in about ten minutes."

"I'll get in the back seat of the station wagon right now," I said, "or can I give you a hand with their baggage?"

"Don't be silly," he said. "If they caught me letting a guest carry baggage, they'd kick me so hard I'd be in orbit around the moon. . . . There's the station wagon over there."

I got in the back seat.

Mr. and Mrs. Wilcox came out in about ten minutes. They were portly Easterners who had been trying to take off weight, get a sunburn and be able to go back East and surprise their friends with a line of horse lingo.

Talking with them on the way in, I learned that they had been at the guest ranch for three full weeks; that while the cowboy boots hurt his feet at first, Wilcox had managed to become accustomed to them so he was now swearing they were the most comfortable boots he'd ever had on in his life; he was going to have rubber heels put on them and wear them every day—"right in the office, by Jove."

I noticed the broad-brimmed sombrero he was wearing, the coat of tan on his face, and felt quite certain that not only would he wear his cowboy boots but he'd manage to find lots of excuses to tilt back in his swivel chair and get his feet up on the desk where awed secretaries and employees could get a good view and realize that their employer was a real old-time, bronc-stomping buckaroo.

Mrs. Wilcox was enthusiastic over the fact that she had taken off seven pounds and "felt like a new woman."

They were so busy talking about themselves that no one talked about me.

When we got to the airport, they checked in their baggage, then went to get breakfast.

I said to Kramer, "What would happen if I didn't go back to the ranch with you?"

"Nothing. Why? You aren't one of these credit risks, are you, Lam?"

"I'm paid up in advance," I said, "and I'd like to have that cabin left undisturbed in case I don't get back tonight."

Kramer looked me over thoughtfully, then gave a quizzical grin. "I thought there was something strange about your restlessness," he said. "I've seen stallions act the same way."

I let it go at that and detoured around to find out when the next plane left for Dallas.

There was one in thirty minutes.

I was on it.

At Dallas, I put in a collect call for Breckinridge.

"Haven't made that settlement yet, have you?" I asked, when he had accepted the charges.

"Not yet, but I'm getting a cashier's check to close the deal. The operator said you were in Dallas."

"That's right."

"What the devil are you doing there?"

"Chasing down some angles on this case."

"Now look, Donald, I don't want to have any misunderstandings about this. If that man has a whiplash injury, we want to settle while we can settle. Actually, he hasn't got an attorney yet but he's threatened to get one. He said he would if it became necessary.

"Now, in a situation of that sort, we settle and we settle fast."

73

"But you haven't settled yet?"

"No. I have a representative going to the guest ranch this afternoon with proper releases all ready to sign. He'll have cashier's checks. We're going to make a very substantial settlement."

"Tell your man to hold off until you hear from me again."

"Why?"

"There's something fishy about this."

"There can be a lot about it that's fishy but he's got a whiplash injury and we're going to have to confess liability. Good heavens, Lam, do you have any idea what it means when you walk into court and have to stand up in front of a jury and say, 'We admit liability. The only question is that of damages'?"

"I know," I told him, "but— When is your adjuster going to get to the guest ranch?"

"He's getting in on the afternoon plane that arrives about three-thirty."

"Okay," I said, "tell him to get in touch with you before he leaves the airport at Tucson. I'll be in touch with you by then."

Breckinridge said, "I like energy, Lam, but there is such a thing as being overzealous."

"I know," I told him, "and there's a damned good chance you're not going to like me because I'm becoming overzealous. That guy, Bruno, is a crook. I'll call you later."

I hung up on that one and left him thinking it over.

I called Bertha Cool, collect.

"What the hell are you doing in Dallas when you're supposed to be at that dude ranch?" she asked.

"Running down a special lead," I told her, "and I've got a hurry-up job for you. There's a registered nurse named Melita Doon. I want a report on her. I particularly want to find out the name of her boy friend. I want to find out where she is staying, whether she's living in a dormitory with nurses, whether she has an apartment, whether she has another girl sharing the apartment with her—in fact, I want to find out all about her."

"What does Melita Doon have to do with this case?" Bertha asked.

"I don't know," I told her. "I want to find out."

Bertha groaned. "Leave it to you to dig up a woman. She's a registered nurse?"

"Right."

"Okay. We'll get busy."

"Don't say anything to Breckinridge," I warned her. "I'll keep him posted on everything he should know." I hung up.

I went into one of the department stores, I purchased a small suitcase, an electric blender and an electric can opener.

I took off all price marks, packed them in the suitcase, then studied the Help Wanted columns of the morning paper. I found one advertising for salesmen on a high-class, dignified, house-to-house presentation which would net a large income.

I went up to the address mentioned and applied for a job.

It was selling a set of encyclopedias.

I said I could do the job, was given some sample brochures, some order blanks and told that after I proved myself I could probably get a guarantee against commissions, but until then I would be strictly on a commission basis. No guarantees, no advances.

I had Helmann Bruno's address, 642 Chestnit Avenue.

I rented a U-Drive car and took my suitcase and samples around. The place was an apartment house, the Meldone Apartments, a pretty fair-looking place.

A check of the mailbox showed that Helmann Bruno was in 614.

I went up and rang the bell.

After a moment, a good-looking woman of about twenty-nine or thirty came to the door.

"Are you," I asked, "the lady of the house?"

Her smile was weary. "I'm the lady of the house," she said. "I've got a dozen things to do and I'm not interested in buying anything. I don't know how you got in here. There's a strict rule against solicitors, peddlers, agents and appliance salesmen."

She started to close the door.

"I'm here," I said, "to give you your free blender and your free electric can opener."

"My what?"

"Your free electric can opener and your free blender."

I put the suitcase down on the carpet in the corridor, opened it up so she could see the blender and the can opener.

"What do you mean 'free'?" she asked.

"Free," I said.

"What do I do in return for these?"

"Nothing."

"Come on, come on, what's the catch?"

I said, "You're the hundred-thousandth prospect for the encyclopedia that I handle, and I have exactly fifteen minutes before I lose out on the prospect and it goes to another salesman. If I can telephone into headquarters that you've signed up within the next fifteen minutes, you get this blender and the can opener."

She laughed and said, "Probably cheap merchandise that won't—"

"Look it over," I told her, handing her the blender. "That would cost you sixty-five dollars anyplace in town. That's the highest quality brand name manufactured."

"Why, so it is. Will it work?"

"Guaranteed."

"Let me see the can opener."

I showed her the can opener.

She hesitated a moment, then said, "Come in."

I followed her into the apartment.

It was a pretty fair-looking place with a sitting room, a half-open door leading to a bedroom, and a small kitchen.

"How much is the encyclopedia?"

"About half what it's worth," I said.

"We have no room for an encyclopedia."

"There's a little bookcase that comes with it, it's printed on thin paper, and you'd be surprised at the amount of accurate information that is packed into it.

"Take, for instance, the question of atomic power and the thrust ratio necessary to overcome the gravitational pull. Scientists refer to it as the critical speed at which a projectile would break loose from the gravitational pull of the earth.

"I can see you're the sort of woman who goes out and gets in circulation. I don't know what educational advantages you've had, but lots of times it pays to impress people with knowledge about some particular phase of a scientific activity which is before the public at the moment. Here, take a look at this reprint of the article on space orbit."

She said, dubiously, "Well, if the encyclopedia doesn't take up too much room and doesn't cost too much, sit down and let me look it over."

She prowled through the reprint pamphlet I had given her on space orbit.

"You see," I said, "this is right up to the minute as far as scientific accuracy is concerned but it's expressed in down-to-earth language that anybody can understand. You could put in half an hour studying that and then stand out in any gathering as a modern woman with a lot of scientific knowledge at your fingertips."

"How much?" she asked.

I said, "We have here a contract and fifty-two easy

weekly payments. When a set is bought on these terms, there is no interest.

"You'll find the encyclopedia is really worth its weight in gold and— I have seven minutes left within which to sign you up. If I do, I'll telephone in to the company and turn over to you gratuitously, without a penny's expense to you, these premium articles which you get for being the hundred-thousandth purchaser.

"Of course, I can't hold the offer open longer than seven minutes more, because there's another salesman waiting at the doorstep of a likely prospect right now, and the minute my fifteen minutes are up, unless he's advised by telephone that I've closed the deal here, I lose my chance at it. The chance then goes to Salesman Number 2. He has fifteen minutes from the time he calls on his prospect in order to close the deal."

"And then?" she asked.

"If he closes it, the prospect gets the premiums. If he doesn't, the opportunity goes to Salesman Number 3, and so on down the line; but at the rate these encyclopedias are selling, with the modern knowledge that they have packed into them, it probably never will get to Salesman Number 3. If you don't close the order here, Salesman Number 2 will almost certainly have his prospect snap it up."

She said, "I like to consult my husband before making purchases like this. . . . Let me see that blender again."

I gave her the blender.

She looked it all over.

"You'll see," I said, "that there's an original guarantee with it, right from the manufacturer. You fill out this postcard and mail it in to the manufacturer. Your blender is registered from that time on. It's guaranteed for a full three years.

"Now, this electric can opener is designed to open any kind of a can; square, round, oblong, anything you put in there. Just pick up the can, push it into this holder, press this button, and the can is opened neatly without any jagged edges.

"Actually, it's against the policy of the company to talk about any premiums we give. We're supposed to sell the books, not the premiums. But we gave smaller bonuses to the purchaser who bought the twenty-five-thousandth set, one to the fifty-thousandth set, one to the seventy-five-thousandth set, and this is an extra bonus with the hundred-thousandth set."

She hesitated.

"When will your husband be home?"

"Not for a couple of weeks, I'm afraid. He's off on a business deal and— Poor man . . . I expect he'll telephone me tonight."

"What's the trouble?" I asked. "Why do you say 'poor man'?"

"He was in an automobile accident. He shouldn't be traveling at all, but this is an important business deal and he had to go."

I looked at my watch and said, "Well, I'm sorry, but if that's the way it is I guess Salesman Number 2 is going to get the bonus customer."

I started putting the electric can opener back into the suitcase, and reached for the blender.

"Wait a minute," she said.

She again looked the electric blender over.

I waited until she had lifted her eyes, then ostentatiously looked at my wrist watch.

"All right," she said, "I'll take it."

"Sign here," I told her, pushing out the contract for the books.

"Heavens, I wouldn't have time to read all this."

"You don't have to," I told her. "You're dealing with a reputable firm. You don't have to pay any money down. Sometime within the next week a person will come and deliver the merchandise. When the delivery is made you make the first payment. Then you make fifty-two equal payments without interest as mentioned right here in this part of the contract. That's the only part that entails any obligation on your part—except, of course, that you represent your credit is good, that you are solvent, that you are not signing this contract with any intention of defrauding the company."

Again I looked at my wrist watch.

She grabbed the pen and signed.

I said, "May I use the phone, please? I only have just a few seconds left."

I dashed over to the phone, dialed a number at random and said, "Hello, hello."

A voice said, "Yes, hello?"

I said, "I'm Mr. Donald and I've made the hundred-thousandth sale. I claim the right to deliver the bonus premiums."

A voice said, "You have the wrong number," and hung up.

I said into the dead telephone, "I have the signed contract. Check with me on time please. . . . That's right, I'm still fifty seconds within the margin. I'm delivering the electric blender and the electric can opener to Mrs. Bruno and I'll bring the contract into the office— That's right, I'm making a delivery now."

I said, "Yes, I have the signed contract," and hung up the telephone.

I picked up the electric blender, took it out to the kitchen, put it on a shelf and said, "There are some screws with which to install this electric can opener. Would you like to have me help you put it up?"

"No, that's fine," she said, "I'll put it up myself. I want to test that blender."

She took off the container, held it under a water faucet, filled it half full of water, put it back on the stand and turned on the blender.

Her smile was ecstatic. "We've been needing one of these," she said. "It seems too good to be true, getting one virtually for nothing this way."

"You're buying the hundred-thousandth set that has been sold to the public on door-to-door canvassing," I said. "When did you say you expected your husband back?"

"Not for two weeks. He's in Minnesota on a business deal."

"Was he injured very bad?"

"One of those whiplash injuries," she said. "At first he didn't think very much of it, but after a while he began to get headaches and dizzy spells and then he went to a doctor, and the doctor diagnosed it as a whiplash injury."

I made clucking sounds with my tongue. "That's too bad. And I suppose the other fellow wasn't insured?"

"No, the other man was insured, but I don't know what the insurance company is going to do about it. My husband is negotiating with them."

"No lawyer?" I asked.

Her eyes were shrewd. "A lawyer would want thirty-three and a third per cent of whatever he recovered. I don't see any reason why a lawyer should cut himself in on something of that sort if we can make our own settlement with an insurance company. There's no reason to pay a lawyer five thousand bucks just for writing a letter and doing a little talking. Heavens, some of those lawyers get rich on good cases like ours. The insurance company sends a representative to their office; they bargain around for an hour or so and then make a settlement.

"Now, it's different if a lawyer has to put up money and file suit and all of that. My husband would be willing to deal with a lawyer on that basis, but no lawyer wants to deal that way. They want to have it understood that they get a third right from the start."

"Well," I said, "I suppose the lawyers have their problems, too. They have to make money on the easy ones in order to enable them to break even on the hard ones."

"All right," she said, "the lawyers can look out for the lawyers, and the Brunos will look out for the Brunos. However, I'm not supposed to discuss the case."

"Why not?" I asked, my eyes wide.

"Oh, you know how it is with insurance companies."

"Oh, yes," I said. "Yes, I can see. Well, perhaps you hadn't better say anything about it then, and I'll be on my way. Thank you very much indeed, Mrs. Bruno. It's a real pleasure to me to be able to deliver the bonus articles. I was afraid for a while there that time was going to run out on us."

She laughed nervously and said, "So was I. My, that's a wonderful presentation on atomic energy and orbiting and that stuff in the encyclopedia."

"You'll enjoy it," I told her, and bowed out.

I went to the office of the encyclopedia company. "What do I do with this contract?" I asked, showing the signed contract.

"You turn it in," the man at the desk said, his voice showing surprise.

I handed in the signed contract. He looked it over carefully.

"That's fast work, Lam. You haven't been on the job more than an hour or two."

"I know," I told him. "I like to work fast."

"Well, you're going to have a real profitable relationship with this company," the man said.

"No, I'm not," I told him.

"You're *not?*"

"No," I said, "there's too much sales resistance to suit me. It took me almost an hour to land this prospect. When I do door-to-door canvassing I like to make at least five sales a day."

"Five sales a day! Do you realize what your commissions would be if you made five sales a day?"

"Of course, I realize what they'd be. I'm in this business to make money and I like to make *real* money."

"You're making it. How many calls did you make?"

"Just this one."

"Only one?"

"Of course. I don't waste time with poor prospects."

"Well, I'll be damned," he said.

He looked at the contract again.

"Look here, Lam," he said, "you didn't check on the credit rating here!"

"Was I supposed to?"

"Well, you guarantee the credit. At least to the extent of your commissions."

"How do you mean?"

"We deliver the encyclopedias. We retain title until the last payment is made. Payments are on a weekly basis. If the payments aren't made, you don't get your commission."

"You peddle your paper, don't you?"

"We peddle the paper, but only after a check has been made on the credit rating and even then we have to stand back of our paper. We have to guarantee it."

I grinned at him and said, "In other words, you have

a subsidiary company which handles the financing and you turn the paper over to it?"

His face flushed, but he didn't make any answer.

"All right," I said, "let's check on the credit rating right now."

He didn't like to do it, but he picked up the telephone, called the credit bureau and asked for a rating on Helmann Bruno at the Meldone Apartments.

I watched his face.

After a few minutes, he frowned and said thoughtfully, "Well, that's okay, I guess."

He hung up and said, "They haven't been there very long, only about three months, but their credit rating is okay. They seem to have cash. They have a bank account, pay by check; have a good automobile that they bought when they came to town, and they pay cash on the barrelhead. On the other hand, no one knows very much about them. Their only charge was for payments on an automobile contract. They say they don't want any credit, so they won't give references."

"That's swell," I said. "I shouldn't have any trouble over commissions then."

"You won't. You won't, Lam, but you should check the credit rating on these customers. . . . Well, that's all right. You've done a good job, a splendid job. Usually it takes a salesman a week or two to get familiar with the ins and outs. My big job is keeping them from getting discouraged."

"I'm discouraged," I told him.

"You—I just can't understand you, Lam."

"I'm easy to understand," I told him. "I'm a guy who likes to make money and I have the line of patter that will make it."

"Well, you sure made a sale in record time on this one. Why don't you stay with us?"

"Not for me," I told him, "I need greener pastures and more lettuce."

"Don't be too pessimistic about this, Lam. Some of our salesmen make very good money, very good money indeed."

"Not my kind of money," I told him. "I'll let you know where to send my commissions on this deal later. In the meantime, here's your advertising matter and samples. I'm picking up something more profitable."

He was flabbergasted as I tossed the stuff on his desk and walked out.

I called Breckinridge again from a telephone booth. As soon as I had him on the line I said, "I wish you'd call off that settlement, Breckinridge."

"What's the matter, Lam?"

"They show too much familiarity with attorneys," I said. "They have had experience with cases of this sort before."

"What makes you think so?"

"They are willing to go to an attorney if suit has to be filed, but they won't touch an attorney with a ten-foot pole if suit doesn't have to be filed. They see no reason for paying some lawyer a third of the settlement just for writing a letter and they figure a third of the settlement will be five thousand bucks."

"Who told you all that?"

"The wife."

"You called on her?"

"Yes."

"You got her to talk?"

"That's right."

"The hell you did! How did you do that?"

"It's a long story," I said. "Of course, she doesn't have any idea I was investigating for an insurance company."

"And you think you're on the track of something?"

"I think I'm on the track of something."

"Well," he said, slowly, "I'll cancel the plane reservation and hold off for one more day, but we're playing with dynamite on these whiplash injuries, Lam, you understand that?"

"I understand all of that," I told him, "but I think you're dealing with a professional."

"That's just a hunch on your part?"

"It's a hunch on my part," I said, "predicated on a little evidence. The guy has a pretty good apartment. His wife is well dressed. They aren't fly-by-nights. They're willing to make an investment in self-improvement, and they don't intend to pay their bills."

"What sort of bills?"

"A set of encyclopedias. They intend to get the books and then move to another address and take another name."

"How do you know that?"

"From the way she signed the contract without reading it."

"You sold her a set of encyclopedias?"

"That's right."

Breckinridge was silent for a moment, then he said, "Lam, you're the damnedest fellow I ever got teamed up with."

"Am I supposed to argue that?" I asked.

He laughed and said, "No."

"All right," I told him, "call off your settlement for a while. I think I can come up with something."

I hung up.

As soon as I had cleared the line, I called Elsie Brand at the office. "Donald," she said, "where are you?"

"This call's going through the switchboard," I said. "Make sure no one's listening in. Step to the door and pretend you're getting some papers out of a filing case. Make sure we have a clear line and then come back."

She was back on the line in about forty seconds. "It's all clear," she said.

"Look," I told her, "I'm coming back to town. I don't want Bertha to know it. I don't want anyone to know it just now. I want to be under cover. How about you telling the manager of your apartment house that you have a cousin from New Orleans who is going to be visiting in town for a few days and would it be possible for him to have an apartment?"

"Well," she said thoughtfully. "Perhaps we could fix it."

"I know you did that with the girl friend who visited

you from San Francisco a couple of weeks ago," I told her.

"That was a girl," she said.

"Be indifferent about me," I said. "Tell the manager you don't want an apartment on the same floor necessarily, just anyplace in the building."

"Well, I'll see what I can do, Donald. What's the trouble?"

"No trouble," I said, "just good old routine, but I don't want anyone to know I'm in town.

"Now, here's something I want *you* to do. I told Bertha about a Melita Doon. I wanted Bertha to find out all about her. By the time I get there, have everything Bertha's found out all ready for me to use."

"When will you arrive?" she asked.

"On American Airlines at five-thirty this evening. Meet me if you can make it."

"Do you know anything about this girl? Where she lives? What she does?"

"Bertha will know all about her by that time. Be sure you get the dope from Bertha's file. It's best if you copy it down."

"Well . . . I'll see what I can do. But I don't like to lie, Donald. You know that."

"I know," I told her, "that's because you don't get enough practice. I'm giving you a chance to practice now so you can have a fully rounded personality."

"Oh, Donald, aren't you ever serious?"

"Never more serious in my life," I told her, and hung up.

Chapter 6

Elsie Brand was waiting for me at the airport.

"Donald," she said, her manner indicating her mental tension, "What's gone wrong?"

"What makes you think anything's gone wrong?"

"You're supposed to be at that guest ranch and Bertha can't understand you leaving there, or all your running around."

"What about Melita Doon?" I asked. "Have we got a line on her?"

"I think so. It's such an unusual name—there could hardly be two people with that name."

"Who is she? What does she do?"

"She's a nurse at the Civic Community Hospital. They were a little closemouthed about her when I tried to find out. We gave the old line about wanting to check on her credit, particularly with relation to her personal habits and all that."

"What did we find out?"

"She had some sort of a nervous breakdown about a week ago and is out somewhere recuperating. They gave her a month's leave of absence. She misfiled some X rays. She's all broken up about it. Got so she couldn't do her work."

"That checks," I said. "But we'd better just check for physical description."

"She's twenty-eight years old, blond, five feet two and a half, weighs a hundred and eight pounds."

"Okay," I said, "that's the one. Who's her boy friend?"

"A man by the name of Marty Lassen. He runs a television repair shop. He's a big, athletic type and he's supposed to be both jealous and short-tempered."

"I always pick guys like that," I said.

"Donald! You aren't going to try to see him, are you?"

"Tomorrow morning, bright and early."

"Oh, Donald! I wish you wouldn't."

"I've got to. Where does she live, and does she live alone or does she share an apartment?"

"No. She shares an apartment. She's in 283 at the Bulwin Apartments, and her roommate is another nurse named Josephine Edgar."

"Know anything about Josephine?" I asked.

"Only that she's a nurse, and evidently a close friend of Melita Doon. They've been living together for a couple of years now. Melita has a sick mother whom she's supporting in a nursing home."

"That checks," I said.

"What about Mr. Breckinridge?" she asked.

"Well," I said, "I'm going to call him right now."

"You have a night number for Breckinridge?" she asked.

"Yes. He said I could reach him there at any time."

I called the number, and Breckinridge's well-modulated, suave voice came over the wire, "Ah, yes, hello, this is Homer Breckinridge speaking."

"Donald Lam," I told him.

"Ah, yes. Where are you?"

"I'm here at the airport."

"You just got in?"

"Yes."

"Lam, I have a hunch about this case, and when I have a hunch about a case it is predicated upon years of long experience and a subconscious appraisal of the situation."

"I dare say it is."

"I have to talk with you."

"Give me your address and we'll drive out," I said.

"Who's the 'we'?"

"Elsie Brand, my secretary."

"I've been trying to get in touch with you at the office. Your partner didn't know where to reach you."

"That's right."

"I felt that I should be able to get in touch with you by calling your partner," Breckinridge said reproachfully.

"Ordinarily you could," I said. "This is something that it may be better if no one knows about. I'll come out and see you if you want."

"Please do that. I'm at my home."

I hung up, and turned to Elsie, "Do you have the agency heap?" I asked.

"No," she said, "Bertha would have wanted mileage and all that stuff so I just took my own car. I felt it would be easier doing it that way."

"All right," I told her, "we're going to run up some mileage on your car."

"Breckinridge?" she asked.

I nodded.

"I think he's quite irritated."

"Probably," I said.

"What do we do?"

"We un-irritate him if possible. I'm sticking my neck way out on this thing and I hope he's willing to ride along. Come on, let's go."

"Could we get something to eat afterwards? I'm starved."

"Afterwards," I promised her, "we'll get eats."

We drove Elsie Brand's car. While we were working our way through traffic, I said, "This is a swank neighborhood, Elsie."

"I don't want to go in with you, Donald. I'll sit in the car."

"Nonsense," I told her. "You met me at the airport, you'll go on in with me."

We drove to an imposing, Spanish-type house with an old-fashioned splendor of trees, grass and a wide porch. To be sure, the lawn was narrow, the trees were closely trimmed, but the house sat back from the street and there was an atmosphere of luxury about it.

I rang the bell.

Breckinridge himself came to the door.

"Well, well, Donald," he said, shaking hands, "you've had quite a day, I guess. And this is your secretary, Elsie Brand? I've talked with her over the phone.

"Come in, come in."

His manner was very cordial.

We entered the house, were escorted into a living room and seated.

Breckinridge didn't sit down. He stood by the fireplace facing me, his hands thrust deep into the side pockets of the cashmere sport coat he was wearing.

"Donald," he said, "I gather that you're rather impulsive, rather quick on the trigger, and once you start work on a case you become very loyal and intensely partisan."

"Is that bad?" I asked.

"But by that same token," Breckinridge went on, "those qualities keep you from following instructions.

"Now, your partner, Mrs. Cool, is pretty much worked up about this quality you have. I'm not nearly so concerned about it because I understand your motivation. However, this case should have been settled by this time. As it is, following your suggestions, we are going to wait until tomorrow. You're now the pitcher responsible for the game. If we lose it's your loss.

"Now, I have no fault with what you've done as far

as factual investigation is concerned, but I permitted myself to be swayed by your importunities into holding this case open for another day.

"I'm sorry I did that.

"I've been in this business long enough so I have a sixth sense in such matters, and I just knew that this was the time to make a settlement and that we should have bought our way out of it, no matter what it cost—that is, within reason, of course."

"All right," I said, "the responsibility is mine. I talked you out of settling. I'm responsible. I don't have any sixth sense in such matters, but I've batted around a bit and there's something fishy about this case."

Breckinridge said, "Even so, Donald, I don't think there's anything we can *prove*. Unless you uncover something before noon tomorrow, I'm going to make a settlement. That's final."

I said, "Apparently you wanted to talk with me just so you could tell me you didn't like the way I'd been doing things?"

He smiled. "Now, Donald, you're getting a chip on your shoulder. Don't be like that. I wanted to tell you how much I appreciated your vigor, your determination, your attempt to get at the bottom of things. In a case where there was any real possibility of a margin of error, all this would have been very commendable but in the present case it simply isn't. You'll have to learn about the insurance business.

"Now, when you see your partner, Bertha Cool, I want you to tell her that you've had a talk with me, that we understand each other perfectly, and that what you have done in this case isn't going to affect our relations with the firm in the least. We're going to keep right on employing you."

"That's fine," I said. "That's mighty generous of you. Now, what makes you so certain that this man, Bruno, is on the level?"

Breckinridge pursed his lips. "Don't misunderstand me. Whether he's on the level or not, the fact that he showed up at that guest ranch complaining of his injuries and getting around in a wheelchair is the determining factor. We can't afford to gamble in a case of that sort."

I said, "You baited one trap and he didn't walk into it. That doesn't make him a saint."

"He walked into the trap," Breckinridge said, "but he walked in limping and he didn't take the bait."

I said, "How carefully have you inquired into the facts of the accident from your insured— What's his name?"

"Foley Chester."

"How carefully have you inquired into the facts with him?"

"Carefully enough so that I know we will have to admit liability."

I said, "Don't you suppose that this man, Bruno, could have been driving, looking in the rearview mirror, watching the car behind him, and the minute he saw the driver look to the side of the road he braked his car to an immediate stop so that Chester *had* to hit him?"

Breckinridge thought that over for a moment and said, "Well, of course that's possible. It *would* be a rather ingenious way of establishing a claim."

"It would be a foolproof way," I said. "There's an attraction on the side of the road, a shopwindow or whatever it was, that has an unusual display. Bruno knows his onions. He realizes this will make drivers look. He drives around and around the block, keeping his eye on the rearview mirror, just waiting for an opportune moment. He sees someone in his rearview mirror who turns to glance at the side and Bruno promptly puts on his brakes.

"There's not much chance of his getting injured very seriously. He's prepared for everything. He gets a bump, he gets out and is affable and good-natured and shows the man behind him his driving license, and the man behind his says, 'I'm sorry. It was my fault. I just took my eyes from the road for a tenth of a second, and there you were stopped right ahead of me.'

"Bruno says, 'Gosh, the fellow in front of me stopped and I had to stop, but I gave a signal and just about the time I came to a stop, *wham*, you hit me.'

"Everything is nice and good-natured and the people get along swell. If Bruno had been abusive, Chester would probably have told him to go jump in the lake, but Bruno is nice, and Chester is very much the magnanimous gentleman and says, 'It's all my fault. You aren't hurt, are you?' And Bruno says, 'No, I'm not hurt.'"

"I don't know much about the accident," Breckinridge admitted. "Chester bought an automobile and insured it with us. He ran into the rear of another car. That's prima-facie negligence per se. Then he admits he wasn't watching the road ahead. That clinches it."

I said, "I'd like to talk with Chester and get his version of what happened, just what Bruno said at the time."

Breckinridge said, "Donald, forget this thing. Good heavens, we're an insurance company. We charge premiums. The premiums go into a sinking fund to cover the payment of losses. We expect to pay out hundreds of thousands of dollars every year. You act as though this was coming out of your own pocket."

I said, "It's the principle of the thing."

Breckinridge frowned. "You mean you're not ready to give up yet despite the fact that I've tried to be patient with you?"

"I'm not ready to give up yet."

He looked at me and flushed, then suddenly laughed a short, harsh laugh. "Donald," he said, "I'm going to prove to you that in this business you can't adopt that attitude. We expect to use you more and more. We've had glowing reports on you from the guest ranch. You have comported yourself with dignity; you've kept in the background, yet you've made people like you. Apparently, you know a good deal about riding a horse, yet you aren't a show-off. You're just exactly the type of person we can use.

"But we can't use you as long as you have that idea about insurance claims and losses. Now, come on, we'll go out to Foley Chester's place right now and talk with him."

"You have his address?" I asked.

"As it happens, I have his address and I know that it's not too far from here, only about three quarters of a mile."

"I've got a car outside," I said, "and we—"

"We'll go in my car," Breckinridge said, with a tone of finality.

Abruptly, a tall, rather angular woman with high cheekbones, black, burning eyes and a determined manner, came striding into the room.

She stopped in apparent surprise and said, "Why, Homer, I didn't know you were having company."

Her eyes slithered very briefly over me and came to rest on Elsie Brand, looking her over from head to toe, the way a certain type of woman will size up a potential competitor.

Breckinridge apparently didn't notice the undertone of hostility and suspicion in her voice. He said easily, "A business matter, my dear. I didn't want to disturb you with it, but permit me to present Miss Brand and Mr. Lam. These people are detectives who are working on a case for us."

"Oh, I see," she said, and smiled acidly. "*Another* female operative?"

"Strictly speaking," Breckinridge said, "Miss Brand is secretary to Mr. Lam. She met him at the airport and drove him out here. . . . I'm sorry, dear, but I'm going to have to leave for a brief interval. We have to interview a witness immediately."

"Oh, I see," she said, and the inflection of her voice was highly significant.

I said to Breckinridge, "Elsie has her car here and there's no need of complicating the situation. You lead the way and we'll follow in her car. Then after the interview you can come back here."

"That probably will be better," Breckinridge said.

"Where are you from, Mr. Lam?" Mrs. Breckinridge asked, slightly mollified. "Where are your headquarters?"

"They're here," I said.

"Oh, I understood Homer to say you came in by plane."

"I did."

"From Arizona?" she asked, and her words were dipped in acid.

Breckinridge gave me a swift, appealing but furtive glance.

"Arizona," I said vacantly. "Why, no, *I* came in from Texas."

"He's been working on a case in Dallas," Breckinridge explained hastily.

"Oh," she said, and her manner was almost cordial. "Well, if you people have to go, you'd better go so my husband can get back."

She bowed to Elsie and me and swept out of the room.

Breckinridge said hastily, "All right, let's get in the cars and go. You people follow me."

We went out a side door. Breckinridge's car was parked in the driveway. It was a big, leather-upholstered, air-conditioned vehicle. He climbed in and slammed the door shut.

Elsie and I walked down the driveway to where her car was parked.

"Why did she act that way about Arizona?" Elsie asked. "She almost spat the word out."

I said, "She's probably a woman of deep-seated prejudices."

"You can say that again," Elsie said. "She has a husband who looks like a matinee idol and she's not sure of him or of herself."

Breckinridge paused as he drew alongside of us. He was consulting a leather-backed memo book which he took from his pocket. He checked an address, turned out the dome light in the car, nodded to us and called out, "Ready?"

"Ready," I said.

I drove Elsie's car. We encountered very little traffic and made good time to a good-looking apartment house.

At the entrance to the place Breckinridge looked at a folded paper; I looked at the directory and said, "He's in 1012. Let's go up."

"Heaven knows whether we'll catch him home or not," Breckinridge said. "I should have telephoned for an appointment, but *you* have *me* acting impulsively now."

We went up in the elevator, found the apartment,

and I pressed the mother-of-pearl button. Chimes sounded on the inside of the apartment.

Nothing happened.

I waited some ten seconds and then rang again.

"Well," Breckinridge said, "he's out. We should have phoned. However, Donald, the principle is the same. I'm going to settle that case tomorrow afternoon."

A door opened down the hall. A man stepped into the corridor, started toward the elevator.

We kept walking on toward the elevator. Out of the same apartment stepped another man, who was just behind us.

The man at the elevator suddenly turned. The man behind us said, "Right this way, please."

Breckinridge whirled. I turned more leisurely. I had heard that tone of voice before.

The man behind us was holding a leather folder with a badge.

"Police officers," he said. "Would you mind stepping this way."

"What's all this about?" Breckinridge asked.

"Right this way, please. We don't care to discuss it in the corridor."

The man who had walked toward the elevator and had turned was now right behind us. He put one hand on Breckinridge's arm, one on mine and pushed.

"Come on, folks," he said. "This will only take a few minutes. Make it snappy."

A door across from us opened; a woman looked out.

The man with the badge said to her, "Never mind, madam."

"What's all this about?" she asked, suspiciously. "What's going on here?"

The officer showed her his badge.

"Well, for heaven's sake," she exclaimed and stood there in the doorway, her jaw sagging, trying to pull her wits together.

The plain-clothes officer escorted us into the apartment from which the two men had emerged.

It was fixed up as a typical police stakeout.

There was a tape-recording machine on the table, a couple of officers seated at another little table, a short-wave radio telephone. The regular furniture of the apartment had been pushed back so that there was room for these new pieces of furniture that had been brought in.

As we entered the room and the door closed behind us, a man stepped out from a closet.

It was Sgt. Frank Sellers, an unlighted cigar in his mouth.

Sellers took one look at me and made an exclamation of disgust.

"Hello, Pint Size."

"Hello, Frank."

Sellers turned to the other officers. "This guy has loused up more cases than any other private eye in the business."

He turned back to me. "What the hell are you doing now?" he asked.

I nodded toward Breckinridge. Breckinridge cleared his throat, said, "Permit me, gentlemen, to introduce myself."

He took out a card case, handed Sellers a card.

"I am Homer Breckinridge," he said, "president and manager of the All Purpose Insurance Company. This is Donald Lam and, I believe, his secretary, a Miss Brand. They are working on a case in which my company is interested. They came to the apartment of Mr. Chester acting on my orders. We want to interview him."

"So do we," Sellers said, studying Breckinridge, looking from him to the card.

"Now this," Sellers said, "can be pretty damned significant. You don't mean Chester's been involved in an accident and you're interested?"

Breckinridge nodded.

Sellers looked disappointed. "And that's why he hasn't come back?"

"I don't know," Breckinridge said. "This accident is one that occurred before he left."

"And he's trying to collect some insurance?" Sellers asked.

"Not at all. He was involved in a very minor traffic accident which, however, has developed into a situation where we would like to talk with him in greater detail than was deemed necessary at the time of his original report."

"Why? Have you got anything on him?"

"Heavens, no. Chester's perfectly all right. He's our insured, but we *are* going to need his testimony."

"Then you're pretty apt to be out of luck," Sellers said.

"What do you mean?"

"Well," Sellers said, indicating the room, "why do you think we've got a stakeout on the place?"

"I haven't the least idea," Breckinridge said. "But I want to find out—and I intend to find out—even if I have to go to the Chief."

Sellers hesitated a moment, then said, "Well, I guess you folks are all accounted for. There's no reason to detain you."

"On the contrary," Breckinridge said with dignity, "I am a substantial citizen and a substantial taxpayer. If there is any police activity involving Foley Chester, I am interested in it and I feel I am entitled to know what it is."

"We're waiting for him to come back," Sellers said. "We think he may have murdered his wife."

"Murdered his wife!" Breckinridge exclaimed, horrified.

"That's right," Sellers said. "We're pretty well satisfied he planned a deliberate premeditated murder."

"Where is his wife?"

"We've recovered her body. It's being held. So far there's been no publicity. We've got to release publicity within the next twenty-four hours or so. We'd like very much to question Chester before we have to face any publicity."

"Oh, my God!" Breckinridge said.

"What's the matter?" Sellers asked.

"Publicity!" Breckinridge exclaimed.

"What about it?"

"The faintest breath of publicity on a charge of that sort and we never will settle the insurance case."

Breckinridge looked at me accusingly. "The price of settlement," he explained to Sellers, "would go up astronomically."

Sellers said, "We're going to sit on it as long as we can, but it'll be bound to break one way or another. Chester took out a pretty good insurance policy on his wife."

"How much?" Breckinridge asked.

"A hundred thousand bucks," Sellers said. "He did it, however, by having his wife insure his life at the same time he insured his wife's life. They called it family insurance and the policy went through all right without arousing any suspicion. In fact, the idea of the policy originated in the mind of the insurance salesman who had called on them and talked about death taxes these days and all of that. He sold them the policies."

"How long was it in force?" Breckinridge asked.

"For over a year," Sellers said, and then added, "If it weren't for what I'm pleased to call some damned brilliant police work, this would have only been a routine case. Chester would have disposed of his wife, taken the money and been on his way."

Breckinridge said to me, "This cooks our goose, Donald."

"Not yet," I said. "Let's remember we haven't heard Chester's side of the case yet."

Sellers said sarcastically, "The boy genius speaks. He knows more about the case than we do and he hasn't even heard the facts yet."

Breckinridge said, "What *are* the facts?"

Sellers said, "After a while, Chester and his wife weren't getting along so well. There were disputes, little altercations here and there. Mrs. Chester decided she was going to San Francisco and told Chester she might never come back. They had quite a scene. Mrs. Chester packed up, went down and loaded the bags in her car. Chester was so mad he wouldn't even help her; he stood and watched. People in some of the other apartments saw it and thought it was pretty damned churlish.

"Then," Sellers continued, "when she'd packed the car, she jumped in, slammed the door, and tried to start the car.

"The car wouldn't start.

"Now, it happens that morning Chester had put *his* car in the garage for repairs and was driving a rented car. Mrs. Chester wanted to take it. Chester wouldn't let her have it. Mrs. Chester went to a drive-yourself car agency, rented a car, arranged to turn it in in San Francisco, arranged with the garage to come and get her car and repair it, and then she was going to fly back and pick it up. She was that mad at Chester, she was getting out of there right then.

"She drove up in the rented car, transferred her baggage, and took off for San Francisco. All of that we know and can prove.

"The next morning Chester turned his rented car in and went to pick up his own car.

"When he turned his rented car in, the people checking it over noticed a couple of places where the paint was off, indicating the car had hit something.

"At first Chester denied he had hit anything. Then he suddenly 'remembered' that he *might* have brushed against a cement gatepost in visiting a friend in the country. He said the scrape had been so slight that he hadn't even noticed it.

"Well, that was a good story but there was a little triangular chip out of the glass on one of the headlights and a little color had rubbed off on the car so that the man who inspected it had an idea Chester had probably scraped against a parked car. He asked Chester about it, and pointed out that Chester was fully covered by insurance, but Chester said that he hadn't anything to report and then apparently, as an afterthought, suddenly snapped his fingers, and said, 'By George, *that's* what happened. I had the car parked and somebody must have scraped against me.'

"So the car rental people let it go at that.

"But Mrs. Chester didn't show up on the appointed date in San Francisco to turn her rented car in. After four or five days the car people began to get nervous. They interviewed Chester, and Chester told them frankly that he hadn't heard from his wife since she left; that as far as he was concerned he didn't give a damn. That she had had two or three affairs since they'd been married; that he was no angel himself but that his wife wanted a double standard. She wanted freedom for herself, but wanted him to toe a chalked line, that he was damned good and sick of it, and, as far as he was concerned, he was just as happy the way things were and he didn't care if she never came back, and since she had signed the contract with the car company, the company could do whatever they damned pleased about it.

"Chester said he was going off on an extended business trip and might not be back for three or four weeks, and as far as his wife was concerned he wasn't going to worry about her, and the car rental people could do the worrying about the car."

Breckinridge said quietly, "We knew in advance that he was going on a business trip but thought he'd be back by now."

"Do you know where he is now?" Sellers asked, becoming suddenly deflated.

"He was going up through the Northwest, up through Oregon, Washington, Montana, Idaho."

"You didn't get an itinerary?" Sellers asked.

"No, we didn't. You see, he had had this accident and he reported it all right, gave us a full statement and we asked him where we could get in touch with him if we wanted an elaboration of his statement. He told us, very frankly, that he was going away, that he had had some domestic trouble, that his wife had left him and probably would file suit for divorce and that was all right by him."

"Okay," Sellers said, losing assurance by the minute, "everything moves along fine and there wouldn't have been anything to it if it hadn't been that this missing rented car showed up wrecked at the bottom of a ravine way down below the Tehachapi Grade. And that would have been all right if the car hadn't caught on fire.

"By the time the car was found, the wife's body was somewhat decomposed, and, if it hadn't been for the fire, would have been *very* decomposed.

"Well, we had a post-mortem on the body and it turned out that Mrs. Chester had been dead before the fire started. The doctor thinks at least an hour before the fire started, perhaps quite a bit longer.

"Well, that was still all right, but we went and impounded the rental car Chester had been driving. They had replaced the headlight and painted over the scratch marks. We went up to the road where Mrs. Chester's car must have gone off and made an inch-by-inch search. We found a piece of glass broken from a headlight. We feel sure it was the piece chipped out of the headlight lens on the car Chester was driving. However, the evidence there is not as robust as we'd like to have it because of the fact that the headlight lens had been replaced. But we can *prove* it's from the same type of headlight used by the company from which Chester rented the car he was driving.

"At the place where we found this broken chip from the headlight, we found tracks in the side of the road off the paved shoulder and in the dirt.

"Those tracks were rather eloquent, despite the fact that some time had passed since they had been made. They told the story.

"Mrs. Chester, making a detour on the Tehachapi, had been forced to the outside of the road. A car apparently had crowded her so far off the road she had lost control. There was a steep slope going down for several hundred feet, then a half-mile slope terminating in an abrupt drop to a dry wash at the bottom.

"Apparently Mrs. Chester had been pushed off the road but had managed to keep from going all the way down the slope, although she presumably was seriously injured. Her husband had calmly parked his car, taken some heavy metallic instrument, probably a jack handle, got out of the car, walked down to where his wife's car had come to a stop, reached in, clubbed his wife over the head until she was dead, and then had taken some time debating what he was going to do.

"He finally decided to destroy any evidence that might be remaining by fire, so he released the brakes, and after a lot of work, got the car started downhill. This time it went clear to the bottom. Then Chester went down and poured gasoline over the car and set fire to it.

"He made one little mistake that betrays him."

"What was that?" Breckinridge asked, an I noticed just a faint trace of skepticism in his voice.

"He left the cap off the gasoline tank.

"He had unscrewed the cap from the gasoline tank,

used a rag of some sort to dip out gasoline, then he squeezed gasoline over the wrecked car and the body. After that he tossed a match into the car and ran. He made his big mistake in waiting to be sure the gasoline in the tank ignited. Having left the cap off the gasoline tank, he forgot to go back and replace it after the fire had burned itself out.

"Once we began to get an idea of what had actually happened, we found a place where the car had rolled over several times and then come to a rest on the side of the hill. We found where someone had gone down to that car and had moved rocks, then used a jack to shove the car around so the wheels would be pointed down hill. Then down at the bottom of the hill we found more tracks again where the man had set fire to the car.

"If that fire had been set at night, it would probably have attracted enough attention from passing motorists to cause a report to the highway patrol. Therefore, we're pretty certain the fire was set during the daytime. But Mrs. Chester left home about four-thirty. She had some people she wanted to see in San Bernardino. We checked there and found that she arrived a little after six, stayed for dinner and left about nine o'clock to drive over the Tehachapi to Bakersfield. Her friends tried to talk her into staying overnight and leaving early the next morning, but she said she liked to drive at night.

"She told her friends that she and her husband were finished, that she didn't want to have anything more to do with him, that she had other interests and there was a man in her life who could fill it a lot more completely than her husband. We can't find out this man's name. It was some cowpuncher she'd fallen for.

"Now then," Sellers said, "that's *generally* the story.

"We're afraid that Chester will skip out if he gets any idea of how much evidence we have, and if he comes back here and gets to nosing around, he'll cross our back trail. Then he'll skip out for good, and we'll have the devil of a time finding him. So we're making a stakeout on his apartment so we can nail him when he comes here, and we want to crucify him by getting his story about his wife leaving him and all of that put on tape. We also want to get him to repeat the story that he either ran into a cement gatepost, or that while the car was parked someone ran into him. We'll get that story put on tape so that we can confront him with it at the trial."

Breckinridge said, without any great enthusiasm, "Sergeant, that makes an impressive array of circumstantial evidence."

"Thank you," Sellers said. "I worked this up mostly by myself—with some help from the office of the Sheriff of Kern County."

"But," Breckinridge went on, "that leaves *us* in the devil of a predicament. We've simply got to settle this accident case before the claimant learns you suspect Chester of murder."

He looked reproachfully at me and said, "After this, Lam, don't ever discount the value of experience. I told you I had a hunch on this case and I've been in this business for years. When I get a hunch, it's right."

He turned to Sellers. "May I go now?"

Sellers said thoughtfully, "I guess so. I guess I can trust your discretion."

"You certainly can," Breckinridge said.

"How about me?" I asked.

Sellers said irritably, "We can trust you to mess the thing up in some way."

"And how about Elsie Brand here?" I asked. "What are you going to do with her? Put her under arrest?"

Sellers scratched his head, worried the cigar around in his mouth, heaved a long sigh and said, "All right, all three of you can go. Get the hell out of the neighborhood and don't have anything more to do with trying to find Chester. Leave that end of it to us.

"Just keep this pint-size troublemaker out of my hair," Sellers said to Breckinridge, "and keep him away from Chester and the whole Chester case. What's the name of the man your insured hit?"

"Helmann Bruno. He lives in Dallas."

"All right, I may want to check on that file," Sellers said.

"Our records are at your disposal any time. We cooperate with the police to the fullest extent."

"Now, of course," Sellers said, "what I've told you about the case against Chester is in strict confidence. The fact that he's suspect probably will come out in tomorrow's papers—perhaps the next day—but right at the moment we want to lead Chester along. We

115

don't want him to know how much we've got on him. We want him to start making a lot of statements that he'll have to contradict later."

"I understand that," Breckinridge said. "I understand police procedure. In fact, we encounter similar problems at times with malingerers."

"Okay," Sellers said. "I'm sorry the boys pulled you in here but that was the plan. We were going to round up any of Chester's friends who came in, particularly if one of them was a jane.

"We don't want any tip-offs to Chester. You'd be surprised what some slick lawyer can think up if you give him time."

"I know. I know," Breckinridge said with feeling. "Believe me, Sergeant, we have the same problems."

The two men shook hands.

Sellers didn't shake hands with me.

Elsie Brand, Breckinridge and I left the apartment and took the elevator down to the street.

Breckinridge said with dignity, "I think, Donald, if your firm is going to represent us in insurance matters, it would be well for you to improve your relations with the police department."

"I'll keep it in mind," I told him.

"Now then," Breckinridge went on, "I'll have an adjuster at that ranch tomorrow. He'll be on the morning plane. I'll have him pay off. We'll probably have to pay a terrific price now, but it'll be worth it. . . . I only wish we'd made the settlement today. I had a hunch on this case."

I said, "We still haven't heard Chester's side of the case."

"We don't need to," Breckinridge snapped.

There was only one thing to do. I kept quiet.

"Now I'm going home," Breckinridge said. "You're relieved of all responsibility in this case, Lam. I'll take it from here—and, by the way, if you ever meet my wife again, don't mention anything about that guest ranch in Arizona. She's sort of prejudiced against it."

That time again I said the only two things there were to say.

"Yes, sir. Good night."

Chapter 7

Elsie Brand said, "I think that Breckinridge person is simply horrid. He doesn't have the faintest sense of appreciation. He doesn't realize that all you've been doing has been for the purpose of saving him money."

I said, "Whoa, Elsie, back up. After all, the guy's the manager of the insurance company. He's the one who's paying the agency for my services. He has the right to expect to have things done his way."

"You feel Bruno is a malingerer, don't you, Donald?"

I thought that one over, then I said slowly, "No, I can't say that I am ready to go that far as yet. I feel that all these people have something phony about them. You get the feeling that they're playing a game.

"I have a feeling that Bruno just *may* be one hell of a smart guy, that he *may* have known that two-week vacation business was a trap, and that this Melita Doon *may* have given him some X-ray pictures that he intends to use later on in the case. I also have a feeling that if Breckinridge had tried to settle earlier today, he just might have found he was running up against a little more of a snag than he had anticipated.

"We haven't enough to go on as yet, but I'm going to see Melita's boy friend, Marty Lassen, in the morning and see if I can get something from him.

"When you suspect a man of malingering and find he's tied up in some way with a nurse, and they are having mysterious meetings, you don't like to quit your investigation until you've ripped things apart.

"But my main feeling in this case is in connection with Chester. I won't say that I'm for Chester because he's the underdog in Sergeant Sellers' doghouse, but because Sellers is inclined— Oh, I don't know, he makes up his mind when the data is about half in. He gets some fellow who's his particular choice suspect and then every bit of evidence that Sellers can get his hands on will point to that person's guilt. He never considers the possibility of innocence."

"Well, you have to admit the circumstantial evidence does look rather black against Chester."

"That's right," I told her, "but we haven't heard Chester's side of the story. When Sellers starts building up a case against someone, every bit of circumstantial evidence he gets hold of has to point directly to the culprit Sellers has picked out, otherwise Sellers thinks it isn't evidence."

"But how can you account for the fact that it was the car driven by Chester which pushed her off the grade?"

"Wait a minute." I said. "How do you know it was the car driven by Chester?"

"Why, the piece from the headlight and the—"

"What you're trying to say is that it may have been the car that was *rented* by Chester that pushed her off the grade, not the car that was *driven* by Chester."

She thought that over for a moment, then said rather weakly, "Yes. When you come right down to it, I guess that's what the evidence does show."

"And," I said, "Breckinridge is founding his whole case, not on a sane investigation of Bruno's claim, but simply on the strength of the fact that his client, Chester, is going to be placed in an untenable position.

"That doesn't mean that Bruno's claim is on the up-and-up, nor does it explain the friendship between Bruno and the nurse who has been connected with a missing X ray."

"Donald, you make it sound so terribly logical that— Well, it *is* terribly logical."

I said, "Look at the crime that Chester is supposed to have committed. He was supposed to have followed his wife over to San Bernardino; then up over the Tehachapi; then pushed her off the grade at a crucial spot; then, when the car didn't roll far enough down to kill her, he parked his car, took an iron jack handle, went down and finished the job, then waited for a while before he decided to push the car down the grade the rest of the way and then, having done that, he waited until daylight and then came back and set fire to the car.

"Now, the way I look at the crime, if you get the real motivation, you find that everything that a person does ties into that particular motivation. Sellers says that Chester was trying to kill his wife in order to get the insurance. Presumably, if Chester is acting in good faith, he doesn't know his wife is dead. If he isn't acting in good faith, he's building up a background so that he can put in his claim against the insurance company and make it appear it's a claim put in in good faith.

"Once his wife was dead, there was no reason for him to push the car all the way down the road to the bottom of the canyon. Once the car and the woman were down at the bottom of the canyon, there was no reason for him to wait several hours and then return to set the car on fire.

"I'm not retained to defend Chester against Sellers' theory, but I am retained to expose any defects in the Helmann Bruno case."

"Well, Donald, I'm betting on you," she said, and reached across to squeeze my hand.

"And you got me an apartment?" I asked.

"There was a vacancy," she said, and then lowered her eyes, "on the same floor. The manager of the apartment was awfully nice about it."

"Well," I said, "I could go for a dinner and, since we have an expense account that—"

"Oh, Donald, Mr. Breckinridge would never stand for a dinner of that sort on the expense account; not after the things that have been happening."

"If Mr. Breckinridge simply saw an account of 'meals,' he'd pay it, wouldn't he?"

"Yes, I suppose so."

"Well," I said, "outside of two glasses of buttermilk, I haven't had anything today and I'm about due."

"Oh, you poor boy," she exclaimed.

"So I take it you'll help me charge the 'meals'?"

"Yes," she said, laughing nervously.

"And," I told her, "how about the 'lodging'?"

She became slightly uneasy. "The manager of the apartment house said she'd put that on my bill. It wouldn't be very much of a charge."

"Then I'll have to manipulate things around so we can get *that* camouflaged on the expense account."

"No, Donald, let me take care of it. I . . . I'd like to feel that you were my guest for once."

"Bertha doesn't know anything about it?"

"Not a thing," she said. "Good heavens, Donald, no one must know anything about it. If they did— Well, Bertha is peculiar anyway. She thinks I can't do my work because I— Well, I mean that I'm supposed to be—"

"I know," I told her. "Bertha has little idiosyncrasies and if she thought that I had occupied an apartment in the same house with you, on the same floor— By the way, where is this apartment?"

"Right across the hall from me," she said.

"No," I told her, "Bertha must never know."

And with that understanding we went to dinner.

Chapter 8

Marty Lassen, a broad-shouldered, powerful giant of a man, about twenty-eight or twenty-nine, was up to his elbows in television repair when I dropped into the place.

"I'd like to talk with you about a personal matter," I said.

He whirled around and sized me up. "What sort of a personal matter?"

"I'm making a security check on a nurse by the name of Melita Doon."

Lassen stiffened like a ramrod.

"It's a routine check," I went on.

"I'd like to find out something about her background, her general characteristics and her reliability."

"Why come to me?"

"I understand you know her. I'm checking with some of her friends. If I don't get the right answers from them, I *may* have to check with her employer."

"What do you mean by the right answers?"

"Those that indicate she's a good security risk."

"Why should she be under investigation for security reasons?"

"There are several different kinds of security," I said.

"Well, why should she be under investigation for *any* kind of security?"

"They pay me to ask questions not to answer them."

"Well, then to hell with you," he said. "You haven't even told me your name."

I smiled at him and said, "That's another thing. Officially my number is S35."

"All right, S35," he said, "you can either walk out under your own power or in about five seconds you can go out with some assistance."

"I'll go out under my own power," I told him. "I'm sorry I bothered you, but I didn't want to go to her employers unless I had to. Sometimes employers get nervous when a security check is being made and it isn't to the benefit of the subject."

"Now, wait a minute, wait a minute," he said, "you aren't going to go messing around asking questions of her employers. Right now that would be fatal."

"Why would it be fatal?"

"Because Melita is having troubles of her own."

"Then *you'd* better help me out," I told him.

"Well, I'm not going to bandy a lot of gossip about the girl."

I looked righteously indignant. "Who said anything about gossip? I simply want to get the background of her character. Where is she now? Do you know?"

"I don't know. She's taking a rest for a few weeks. They— Well, they gave her a lay-off."

"She's a nurse?"

"Yes."

"A trained nurse? Registered?"

"Yes."

"Thoroughly trustworthy?"

"Absolutely."

"Wasn't there some trouble at the hospital where she was employed?"

"You're damned right there was," Lassen said. "There's a supervisor over there who has it in for her, and the kid got blamed for things that she had nothing to do with."

"Such as what?"

"A couple of times X-ray photographs have been lost, and an examination of the files shows that several additional X rays are missing. That could happen anywhere, any time. Dozens of people have access to those files, particularly doctors who are notoriously careless."

"They blamed that on Melita?"

"They blamed it on Melita. They were just looking for an excuse to give her a bad time. Then this patient walked out on her and they want Melita to pay the bill."

"What do you mean he walked out?"

"It wasn't a 'him.' It was a 'her.' They have them once in a while in any hospital. A patient will be on the road to recovery, know that there's a big bill she'll have to pay and will pretend that she's not doing quite so well as she really is. Then in the middle of the night she'll get up, dress and tiptoe out of the place."

"Can they do that? I thought the night nurses were on duty at a desk where—"

"Sure they can do it if they know the hospital. There are all kinds of exits. They can take the stairs up to the laboratory or down to the X-ray room. They can go out through the ambulance entrance or they can ring the bell to call the night nurse and run around the L in the corridor and wait out of sight. Then when the nurse enters the room they can dart down the stairs and be on their way."

"What about this case?"

"This case wouldn't have been important if it hadn't been for their hatchet-faced supervisor and the fact they were already giving Melita a bad time over those missing X rays. This supervisor is picking on Melita and trying to make her quit.

"Actually, I think this supervisor is responsible for the whole thing, the missing X rays and everything, and is looking for a patsy.

"Anyway, they're trying to make Melita pay the hospital bill on the walkout. It's nearly three hundred dollars and that's more than the kid can scrape up.

"She has a sick mother she's supporting and— Well, I told her to tell the hospital I'd guarantee the bill, but she says it's a matter of principle with her and she won't pay them a cent. She says that if she does they'll consider it an admission she's responsible for those missing X rays and this hostile supervisor will really clobber her."

"They have walkouts from time to time?" I asked.

"Of course they do."

"What about this one?"

"It was a woman who was a professional goldbricker. She was young, early thirties, and as it turned out she didn't have any connections anywhere. She'd been divorced from her husband, and her boy friend washed his hands of the whole transaction. She was ready for discharge, then apparently she'd taken a turn for the worse, but that was just an act she put on. About midnight she got up, took her clothes out of the closet and sneaked out. There's a two-hundred-and-seventy-eight-dollar hospital bill and they want Melita to pay it; they claim it was her fault. It's thrown her on the verge of a nervous breakdown. It's really the fault of the Admission Department. This woman was a goldbricker who knew the ropes. She talked the Admission clerk into accepting a no-good check.

"Therefore, you can see what a hell of a mess you'd stir up if you went to the hospital now checking on Melita for security reasons."

"Do you know where Melita is now?"

"I have a good idea."

"Where?"

"That," he said, "is something I'm not going to tell unless I have to. I don't want her to be bothered."

I thought things over for a while and said, "Well, I guess you're probably right at that. Understand, Mr.

Lassen, our department tries to get information that's dependable and reliable, but we don't go around working hardships.

"Now, I have another name here, and my people weren't certain you knew him, but they're checking on him, too. Helmann Bruno, what do you know about him?"

"Bruno? Bruno?"

"That's right. Helmann Bruno."

Lassen shook his head, "Never heard of him."

"Some sort of a manufacturer's agent, or something. Does a good deal of traveling."

Lassen again shook his head.

I asked him about four or five other names that I'd picked at random from the telephone directory. Lassen didn't know any of them.

I said, "That's strange. There's just a chance that Melita's name may have been included in this list by mistake. Don't say anything about it to anyone."

"*I* won't say anything about it," he said belligerently, "but *you* be damned careful *you* don't say anything that would get around and hurt her."

I smiled at him and said, "I'll repeat, my function is to get information, not to give it. Thank you very much indeed, Mr. Lassen."

I turned abruptly and walked out. I turned at the door to see him standing there looking at my back with a somewhat puzzled expression.

Then the piled-up work claimed his attention and he went back to repairing television sets.

Chapter 9

It was hard to get Bertha to betray surprise, but when I walked unannounced into her office, she showed surprise, consternation and then anger.

"What the hell are *you* doing here?" she asked.

"I flubbed the job," I said.

"What do you mean?"

"I ranked it."

"Don't use that damned underworld slang with me," she said. "Rank is a word safe-crackers use when they've used too much nitro and blown the safe all to hell."

"That's the point," I said, "I've used too much nitro. I've blown things all to hell."

"What happened?"

I said, "Breckinridge wanted to settle. I talked him out of it. I told him I thought Bruno was a phony. Now, the price has gone up, due to circumstances I couldn't anticipate."

"And Breckinridge blames you."

"Breckinridge is disappointed."

"Damn it, Donald," she said, "that's the worst of you. You're a brainy little cuss but you're too damned conceited. You have squeezed through so many situations by sheer luck and mental agility that you think the world is your oyster."

"The world isn't my oyster," I said. "The world is pretty grim at the moment. If Breckinridge calls up and asks where I am, you don't know."

"I can't tell him that," Bertha said. "I—"

"The hell you can't," I told her. "If you don't know, that's what you'll *have* to tell him."

"What are you doing in the office?" she asked.

"I came to get our camera," I said. "I want to take some photographs of the scene of an accident."

"You mean you're going all the way back to Texas? Why, the scene of that accident is nothing. As I understand it, it was just a plain street, that's all there is to it and the accident is long gone and over with."

"I didn't say I wanted to photograph the accident," I said, "I said I wanted to photograph the *scene* of the accident."

I walked out; went to my office and met Elsie Brand's troubled gaze.

"How was she, Donald?"

"She's a little flabbergasted at the moment. She'll snap out of it pretty quick and get on the warpath. I'm on my way, wish me luck."

Elsie Brand smiled with her lips and her eyes. "Luck, Donald," she said tenderly.

I grabbed a camera and some films, went out and

drove to the Bulwin Apartments and rang the bell on
283.

A remarkably good-looking, cool-eyed young woman
about twenty-eight or twenty-nine opened the door and
surveyed me with frank interest.

"Well, hello!" she said. "We don't ordinarily get
salesmen of your type. Don't tell me you're working
your way through college getting subscriptions to magazines?"

Her smile was challenging.

"What sort do you usually get?" I asked, matching
her informality of banter.

"Older men who have lost the security of jobs and
have to take up door-to-door peddling on a commission
basis. I feel sorry for them but if I bought all the stuff
they have to peddle I'd be broke flatter than I am now,
and that's plenty flat."

"May I come in?" I asked.

"You want to?"

"Yes."

"Come on."

She opened the door invitingly.

It was a much larger apartment than I had anticipated. There was a comfortable well-furnished sitting
room, two doors at each side, both opening into bedrooms; a kitchen in the back. Apparently each bedroom
had a bath.

"Want to sit down before you start your sales
pitch?" she asked.

"Do I have to start a sales pitch?"

Her eyes were cool and smiling. "*All* men have a sales pitch," she said.

"I'm not selling," I told her. "I'm **trying to get information.**"

"About what?"

"About a person, a Melita Doon; a nurse who is supposed to be living here. Is she home?"

"I'm Miss Doon," she said. "I'll answer any questions you have. What are you looking for?"

I said, "The description I have indicates that Miss Doon is entirely different. I would gather that you are Josephine Edgar, her roommate."

She laughed and said, "Well, it was a good attempt. I was trying to protect Melita as much as possible. I thought if I could answer the questions it would save her a lot of bother.

"What's it all about?"

"Just a routine check," I said.

"How come?"

"I want to find out something about her, her background, her credit rating."

"What's your name?"

"I have a number," I said. "S35."

Her eyes suddenly became hard and cautious. "What governmental department are you in?" she asked.

I said, "Circumstances make it inexpedient for me to identify myself, other than the fact that I am S35."

"Are you, or are you not, in a governmental service? Now, Buster, I'm asking that question to put you right on the spot, because I'm going to do a little investigating of my own."

"I am not in the governmental services," I said.

"You're an investigator?"

"Yes."

"A private detective?"

"Yes."

She extended her hand. "Give."

"What?"

"Your credentials."

I shook my head and said, "I'll just be known as S35, if you don't mind."

"I do mind," she said. "You want to find out something about Melita. Your only way of finding out is to put your cards on the table and to be frank—otherwise I walk over to that telephone, put through a long-distance call to Melita Doon and tell her that private detectives are on her trail."

"You may do that anyway," I told her.

"I may," she said, "but I wasn't born yesterday."

I took out my wallet and showed her my credentials.

"Donald Lam," she said. "That's a nice name. What do you want to know, Donald?"

I said, "Specifically, I'm interested in finding out about the trouble Melita had at the hospital. Was it her fault?"

"Was it her fault?" she echoed, her voice rising in a crescendo of emotion. "It was the fault of that damned Howard hussy, the hatchet-faced superintendent who has been doing nothing but making trouble for Melita ever since she came on the job.

"And now she's gone so far as to accuse Melita of stealing X-ray photographs and she's just about forced the kid into a nervous breakdown."

"What about the X rays?" I asked.

"She wouldn't have dared to do anything like that if it hadn't been for the walkout," Josephine said. "The walkout triggered the whole situation. It gave that Howard woman just the opportunity she wanted.

"Of course, the walkout was partially Melita's fault, but only partially. We all have walkouts from time to time—that is, most of us do. I've had one and I know other nurses who have had them.

"And I'll tell you this, Donald Lam, we don't have a walkout if the front office is on the job. When the patient comes to the receptionist, the receptionist should be able to segregate the legitimate ones from the deadbeats and the goldbrickers. If they'd do a good job, we wouldn't be bothered with walkouts.

"But what happens?

"Some goldbricker with a smooth line of gab—usually a woman—peddles a hard luck story, makes promises and gets admitted. Then if it's a surgical case she can't be bothered too much and she pretends she's not doing so well when actually she's getting along all right.

"However, I've had walkouts get up and leave after surgery when it was actually dangerous for them to go. Well, I say I've had walkouts; I mean the one walkout

I had. It was a surgical case and she left the day she was given bathroom privileges."

"But what about the X rays?" I asked.

"Nothing to it," Josephine said. "She had the walk-out, all right, but the X rays she had nothing to do with. They were simply films that were missing from the files.

"And there again it's always someone else's fault. The person in charge of the X-ray department is supposed to get some sort of a record when X-ray films are taken from the files, but it just happens that in this instance the little nitwit who has charge of the X-ray department is a particular friend of this Howard woman and no one would try to hold her responsible for anything, oh, dear no! She's the teacher's pet.

"No one would ever accuse that girl of letting a doctor take out a bunch of X rays without signing up. No one would ever accuse her of putting X rays in the wrong envelopes after some doctor had had them out looking at them, or taking them up to a room to show them to the patient.

"So it's Melita who gets the thing in the neck, and I'm just downright mad about it."

"Going to do anything about it?" I asked.

"I don't know," she said. "Sometimes I think I'd like to go down there and snatch that Howard woman bald-headed."

"You don't work in the same hospital?"

"I'm on special," she said.

"Night or day?"

She shrugged her shoulders and said, "Any time."

"Keep you pretty busy?" I asked.

"Off and on," she said vaguely.

"Melita has a sick mother?"

"I'll say she does. She's keeping her mother in a nursing home and it's bleeding the girl white, but it's the only thing that can be done and Melita just works her head off.

"Of course, she gets some professional courtesies from doctors, but her mother had to have an operation and Melita had to put up money. That's one of the reasons that this hatchet-faced superintendent tried to lower the boom on Melita. She knew that Melita was up against it for money."

"Well," I said, "I guess that covers all I need to know. Thanks a lot."

I got up to go.

Josephine came over to stand close to me. "Donald," she said, "what are you *really* after?"

"What do you mean?"

"Who's interested enough to ask you to make a checkup on Melita?"

"It's just a routine checkup," I said.

"Who's your client?"

"Heavens," I said, "I don't handle the business end of the office, my partner does that. I get out on the firing line and make the investigations."

"You could be working for that Howard woman for all you know?"

"I could be, for all *you* know," I told her.

She pouted and said, "You're not being a bit nice, Donald."

She moved even closer. "Donald, tell me," she said.

"Tell you what?"

"Who your client is, and why this investigation?"

I said, "You're trying to get me to betray my solemn obligations and you're using sex in order to get me to do it."

She looked me straight in the eyes. "I haven't used it *yet*," she said.

I said, "You're weakening my wall of resolution, woman."

She put her hands on my shoulders, pushed her body close to mine. "Donald, tell me, is Melita going to get into any trouble?"

"Why should she get into any trouble if she hasn't been doing anything wrong?" I asked.

"I just don't trust that Howard woman. I have a feeling that there's something going on in that hospital, that the Howard woman is mixed up in something pretty deep and she's trying to use Melita as a patsy."

"Well," I told her, "I'm making a fair investigation."

"Donald, will you do one thing?"

"What?"

"Will you let me know what you find out when you get all finished?"

"Perhaps."

"Donald, I mean it. I'd be . . . very grateful . . . very, very grateful, Donald."

"I'll see," I promised, and with that, left the apartment.

Josephine stood in the door watching me down the corridor. When I was at the elevator she blew me a kiss, then stepped back into the apartment and gently closed the door.

I telephoned the office and got Elsie Brand.

"Elsie," I said, "call Dolores Ferrol at the Butte Valley Guest Ranch and ask her if Melita Doon had a long-distance call which came in between now and the time you talk with Dolores on the telephone.

"You can catch her at two o'clock. It'll be right after the lunch hour and just before the people go to siesta. She has a little free time then.

"Tell Dolores who you are, and tell her that you're calling at my request, that I'll be seeing her shortly, and tell her to keep the inquiry confidential."

"Okay," Elsie said. "Where are you going?"

"I'm headed for Tehachapi right now," I told her. "I'll be back sometime late this afternoon."

Chapter 10

I took my camera, some films, and drove up to Tehachapi.

It wasn't too difficult to locate the scene of the accident. The police had winched the wrecked car up the hill, and since the tires had been burned off the car, the operation had left quite a furrow. Finding any clues to indicate what had originally happened wasn't so easy. Tracks had been obliterated.

I followed the detour and picked the place where I *thought* Mrs. Chester's car had been crowded off the road. There were tracks indicating that the car had gone end over end down the steep slope for about two hundred yards, then had come to a stop against a big rock. There were bits of broken glass around this rock and places where the paint had scraped off the car.

Studying the tracks, it became evident that someone had wanted the car a lot farther down the hill than it was and had apparently taken a jack and pushed the rear end of the car around so that it cleared the rock and started on down the hill again.

This time the car took a long, erratic journey.

The hill was a good forty-five-degree slope and it went down and down and down, until finally it hit a place where the bottom of the hill terminated in virtually a straight drop of fifty or sixty feet down into a sandy canyon.

Police had been all over the place and had evidently taken lots of pictures. There were burnt-out flashbulbs lying on the ground as well as cigarette stubs and all sorts of shoe tracks, both at the place where the car had crashed against the rock and then farther down the hill at the bottom of the canyon.

It took me five or ten minutes to find the tortuous path down the rocky wall so that I could get up to the place where the car had finally come to rest.

Police apparently had winched the car right straight up the side of the rocky wall, letting the car scrape against the rocks, and then had hoisted it completely up the hill to the highway where they must have loaded it on a truck and taken it down to the county seat.

Apparently there must have been evidence in the car which the police thought it would be wise to perpetuate.

Raising that car up must have taken a lot of cable, a lot of power and been rather an expensive operation— the police really wanted that car, or what was left of it.

The place where the car had been crowded off the road was way up at the top of a high, steep mountain that was studded here and there with rocks but for the most part, covered with a smooth dried grass and stunted sagebrush which is so characteristic of certain hills in Southern California.

After that high place, the road wound on down the mountains, at places winding way back from the canyon, then circling around a ridge and coming back until, looking down the bottom of the sandy wash, I could see where the road came to within a few yards of the termination of the canyon—a distance of perhaps a mile or so.

I studied the terrain carefully, then started walking down the sandy bottom toward the mouth of the wash.

The sides became less precipitous and after a while I ran out of tracks. Police hadn't gone down the canyon this far.

There were still steep rocky sides, not quite so high, but covered here and there with sagebrush and it was difficult working my way along, but I stayed with it for a few hundred yards.

At length I came to a place where there were tracks still visible in the sand.

It had been some time since those tracks were made, but there they were.

They were a man's tracks, a man who wore shoes, but in that dry, coarse sand there wasn't enough shape to them for me to find any marks of identification.

About half a mile down the sandy wash, I came to a place where someone had tossed away the stub of a half-smoked cigarette.

I picked it up with the point of my knife, put it in a

141

little cardboard box I had brought along just in case, and was following the tracks on down the wash when a rock rolled down from above me.

I looked up.

Frank Sellers and another man were working their way down the steep slope.

"Hold it, Pint Size," Sellers said.

I stopped.

The men came on down. The man with Sellers had a badge showing he was a Kern County deputy sheriff. He was fifty and heavy.

Sellers jerked his thumb, said, "This officer is Jim Dawson, a deputy of the Kern County Sheriff's office. Now what the hell are *you* doing up here?"

"Looking over the scene of the crime," I said.

"Why?"

"I'm checking."

"Checking what?"

"Checking your conclusions."

"I told you to keep the hell out of this," Sellers said. "We don't need any of your help."

"I'm not so certain," I told him.

"What do you mean by that crack?"

I said, "You notice these tracks going down the wash way below the place where the car was burned?"

"What about them?"

I said, "Somebody walked down along the side of the barranca until he reached a point where he felt sure no one would be looking for tracks, then he came on down the sandy wash here."

"You're nuts!" Sellers said. "Foley Chester pushed his wife off the road up there at the dirt detour. He left his car right up there within a hundred feet of where she went off the road, then he climbed back up, got in his car and drove away. We've got the deadwood on him. We've got the tracks and we've got photographs to prove it."

"Then who is the man who walked down the barranca here?"

"I don't know and I don't care," Sellers said. "All I know is that we've been setting traps all over, stakeouts waiting for Chester to come walking in and you keep going around springing those traps. We can't afford to have you do it. We're going to clip your wings. What've you got in that box?"

"A cigarette I picked up a hundred yards from here. It's a half-smoked cigarette, and you can make a classification test on the saliva. There may even be a fingerprint or—"

Sellers grabbed the box, opened it, took a look at the cigarette stub, said, "Baloney! You and your goddam theories!"

He threw the stub away.

I said, "You'll wish you hadn't done that, Sellers."

The Kern County deputy wasn't a bad egg. "Look here, Lam," he said, "you've got an interest in this case. Now, why not put your cards on the table?"

"I'll put them on the table," I said. "Foley Chester had an automobile accident. It was his fault. The guy who was injured will hold up the insurance company for an exorbitant settlement once he gets the idea Chester is wanted for murder.

"If Chester killed his wife, that's one thing. If he didn't, it's another. I want to find out which it is before I have to make a settlement.

"So far you've got circumstantial evidence. It points to Chester. I want to find out if you've got *all* the evidence.

"The only way to evaluate circumstantial evidence is to be sure you have *all* the circumstantial evidence."

The deputy was nodding his head.

Sellers said, "Oh, forget it, Jim. You listen to that guy talk and he'll make you think there never was any corpse, never was any burnt car, never was any scraped paint, never was any evidence."

I said, "Foley Chester goes out on business trips. While he's gone he leaves no forwarding address. There's nothing to indicate this isn't one of his regular business trips. You have some scraped paint on a car that he rented, and a chip from a headlight by way of evidence and that's just about all."

"Go on," the deputy said. "If you have any theories, we'd like to hear them."

I said, "All right, you folks went down there in the canyon to look at that burnt automobile."

"Right."

"But," I said, "according to the tracks, you didn't walk down this sandy wash."

"Right again."

"Therefore, you must have climbed back up to the highway."

"Right the third time."

"How long did it take you?"

Dawson grinned and ran his hand over his forehead. "I'm not as good at that stuff as I used to be," he admitted. "I damned near passed out before we got there. I was huffing and puffing up that slope. It seemed like hours."

"Did it take a half an hour?" I asked.

"It took all of that," he admitted.

"All right," I told him, "where that car went off the road it's on a curve and the road is relatively narrow."

"Sure," the deputy said, "it had to be that kind of a place where he elected to push her off, because if there hadn't been a curve and the road hadn't been narrow, she could have dodged, put on her brakes, gone ahead or something and kept from getting pushed off right at that particular place where the car would go all the way on down."

I said, "Your theory is that the car was pushed off there. That it rolled down part way and came to a stop against a big boulder. That Chester stopped his car, went on down with a jack handle, clubbed his wife to death, took a jack, presumably out of his own car, jacked the rear end around so that it was clear of that rock it was resting against, then sent the car rolling down to the bottom of the canyon, a long, long, long ways down."

"That's right."

"Then he climbed back to his car and went someplace waiting for it to get daylight. When it got daylight, he came back, parked his car, climbed on down to the wreck, soaked rags with gasoline, left the cap off the gasoline tank and set fire to the wreckage."

"Anything wrong with that?" the deputy asked.

"Then," I said, "he must have climbed back up to his car."

"That's the way we figure it," the deputy said.

Sellers spat on the ground.

"Then," I said, "he must have left his car parked up there on that narrow curve in the detour for something like an hour and a half. You notice those signs that say, NO STOPPING. PARKING FOR EMERGENCY ONLY and all that. How long do you think you could leave a car parked up there on that curve without somebody reporting it to the traffic officers, or some traffic officer coming along and giving you a tag?"

Dawson said, "Say, you just *may* have something there."

He turned to Sellers. "Let's take a look at the traffic citations. There's just a chance we've been overlooking a bet here."

Sellers said wearily, "Don't listen to him, just don't listen to him. You see that road up there?" he asked the deputy.

"Sure," the deputy said.

"All right, you listen to Lam and pretty quick you'll be believing that it isn't a road at all, that it's just a piece of thread that got stuck to your eyeglass and

146

you're looking at it with your eyes out of focus and think it's a road."

He turned to me and said. "You always have lots of theories, Pint Size. Sometimes they're okay but this is once we don't need them. This time we've got the deadwood. We know what we're doing. We've got all the evidence we need to convict. What we need now is the defendant. We're more interested in an arrest than in a dissertation on circumstantial evidence."

I said, "Circumstantial evidence is not so hot unless you have *all* the circumstances. The tracks leading down this sandy wash are part of the circumstances you haven't had. That cigarette is part of the evidence you haven't had. The murderer couldn't afford to take a chance on leaving a car parked up at that dangerous section on the detour."

"He *could* have gone on down the grade half a mile and left the car there," Sellers pointed out.

"He could have," I said, "or he could have had an accomplice who drove the car down the grade. Then all the murderer had to do was to walk down this sandy wash until he came to the place where the grade crosses the wash. It's a matter of about a mile walk on fairly easy going as opposed to a half hour's climb in the beating sunlight."

"Okay, okay," Sellers said wearily. "He had an accomplice. After we get him, we'll get a confession and we don't give a damn whether he had an accomplice or not. What we want is to get him."

I said, "You go ahead and build up a murder case

against Foley Chester in his absence, then Chester shows up and you have a surprise for him, a nice fat murder rap."

"I'll say we have a surprise for him," Sellers said.

"Who knows," I pointed out, "by the time he gets back you may have distorted the evidence enough so that the guy can't prove his innocence."

"What evidence?" Sellers asked sarcastically.

"The evidence of this man walking down the sandy bottom of the barranca, for one thing," I said. "Figure it out for yourself. The road is coming down a steep ridge. It makes half a dozen loops, but it comes back within a hundred feet of this sandy wash not over a mile and a half down there from where you found the car, and even if you only go half a mile down the wash, the elevation is decreased so that it's only a couple of hundred yards back to the road.

"If I had gone down to burn up a car, I wouldn't go climbing back up that steep slope. I wouldn't leave a car up there where any traffic officer would tag it and question me. I'd set fire to the wrecked car and then I'd walk down the sandy slope of the barranca."

"And then walk back along the road to the car?" Sellers asked dryly.

"Not if I had an accomplice," I said.

The deputy turned to Sellers questioningly.

Sellers made a gesture of dismissal, waving his hand at the same time giving a bronx cheer.

I said, "That cigarette is a brand you don't hear of very often, and doesn't do any advertising. It relies on good tobacco. And, if you're lucky and the evidence hasn't been handled too much, you can get a blood type from the saliva."

"Phooey," Sellers said.

The Kern County deputy walked over to where Sellers had thrown the cardboard box and the cigarette, looked down at it for a moment, then picked it up and put it back in the cardboard box; put the cardboard box in his pocket.

"Let's not overlook any bets that the defense could capitalize on," he said. "Now that Lam has pointed this out, some defense attorney might claim we'd botched up the evidence."

"Now that Lam has pointed it out, is right," Sellers said. "Lam, you get in your automobile and get the hell out of here, and don't hang around *any*place where Chester is apt to be until we've put the cuffs on him. Now, I mean that. That's a lawful order given you by an officer of the law. You keep the hell away from Chester and from the places where he's apt to be.

"And now," he went on with elaborate sarcasm, "since we know how busy you are, there's no need to detain you. You can just get on about your business. . . . And, if you trigger one of our stakeouts so that Foley Chester gets wise, so help me, I'm going to take a rubber hose and give you a working over that you'll remember to your dying day. Now, get started!"

I looked in Sellers' eyes and I got started.

Jim Dawson, the Kern County deputy, was watching me thoughtfully as I climbed up to the road.

Chapter 11

From a telephone booth I called the Butte Valley Guest Ranch and asked to talk to Dolores Ferrol.

It took me a minute to get her on the phone. I could hear music and laughter.

"Hello, Dolores," I said. "Donald Lam talking. What did you find out about Melita Doon?"

"Why, Donald, I talked with your secretary this afternoon and—"

"That's all right," I said, "I told her to call you. But, what about Melita?"

"The strangest thing happened," she said. "Melita got a telephone call sometime before noon. I don't know exactly when it was, but it came in while I was out on the morning ride."

"And what happened?"

"She packed up in a hurry, said her mother was worse, that she had to leave. By the time I returned from the horseback ride, she was gone. It was that fast."

"That's fine," I told her.

"Donald," she said, "people have been asking questions about you."

"That's all right," I told her. "Let them ask. I'm just checking up."

"Don't stay away too long," she said, in the seductive voice of the professional courtesan.

"I won't," I told her and hung up.

It was nearly seven o'clock when I checked in at the office to put the camera back in the closet and see if there were any notes on my desk.

There was a light in Bertha's office.

She evidently heard me come in and jerked the door open.

"My God," she stormed, "trying to keep in touch with you is giving me ulcers from my Adam's apple down. Why in hell don't you tell me where you're going?"

"Because I didn't want anyone to know."

"By anyone, I presume you mean Frank Sellers."

"That was part of it."

"Well, Frank Sellers knew all right. He called me up and said if you didn't keep your nose out of that murder case he was going to throw you in the can and keep you there until the case was settled."

"Frank is impulsive," I said.

"Also he was mad as hell."

"He gets mad," I said. "It's a weakness in an investigator."

"Homer Breckinridge is anxious to see you," Bertha said. "He's been calling every half hour— Here he is

151

now, I guess," she interpolated, as the phone rang.

She picked up the phone and instantly her voice changed to honey and syrup.

"Yes, Mr. Breckinridge, he just this minute came in the door. I was going to tell him to call you—he hasn't been in here ten seconds . . . yes, I'll put him on the phone."

She handed me the telephone. Breckinridge said, "Hello, Donald?"

"That's right."

"There's hell to pay."

"What's the matter?"

"I guess I outsmarted myself."

"How come?"

"It seems that this man, Bruno, was a lot smarter than we gave him credit for being."

"What happened?"

"Well, it seems that Alexis Melvin is in on the case."

"Who's he?"

"Alexis Bott Melvin is a whiplash injury specialist who is hated and feared by every insurance company in the West."

"He's that good?" I asked.

"He's that bad," Breckinridge said.

"And what has he done?"

"He's moved in on the case.

"Now, I can't tell whether Bruno was wise all along or whether Melvin was the one that got wise and has been giving us lots of rope so we would hang ourselves good and hard."

"Go on," I said.

"I can't very well explain it to you over the telephone. I would like to talk with you tonight, but I can't leave my house at the moment."

"Do you want me to come out there?"

"If you could, Donald, it would be a big help."

He hesitated a moment, then went on, "I am alone at the moment. My wife may come in while we are here. In the event she does, I think it would be best to be vague about details. There are some things about this business that she doesn't understand."

"I understand," I told him.

"Thank you, Donald. You've shown great tact. You understand that it is necessary in this business to work with female operators just the same as it is necessary in your business, but it is always difficult to explain these matters to a woman."

"I understand perfectly," I said. "I'll be out in about an hour. There's one matter I have to take care of first. I can't make it before that, but you don't need to worry, you can trust my discretion."

His voice showed relief. "Thank you, Donald. Thank you ever so much."

I hung up. Bertha was watching me with shrewd, glittering eyes.

"What have you done to that man?"

"Why?"

"You've hypnotized him. He was pretty much put out earlier in the day but then he got some phone calls from an agent somewhere. It looks as though they've caught him with his hand in the cookie jar and he's certainly yelling for help now. He wants to talk with you and he says it's so confidential he can't even tell me what it is he wants to talk with you about. He says you'll understand, but that it would take too much explanation for me to get the picture."

I grinned at her and said, "Perhaps things will work out all right after all."

Bertha said, "That secretary of yours said there was a note under your blotter that you should read as soon as you came in."

"Important?" I asked.

"She probably thinks it's important. She thinks anything you do is important. She left word with the switchboard operator to let her know immediately if you called in."

"Okay," I said, "I'll take a look under my blotter, see what it's all about and then run out to see Breckinridge."

"And then what?"

"Then I don't know," I said. "We'll see how things are shaping up."

"Did we get all the dope on that little nurse you wanted?" Bertha Cool asked.

"Not quite," I said. "I talked with her boy friend this morning and then I talked with her roommate."

"What did you find out?"

"She's been accused of stealing X-ray photographs that show injuries and presumably peddling them out to persons who are malingering."

"Don't those X-ray photographs have key numbers on them that show where they came from?"

"Sure," I said, "but they can get around that. They copy the part of the X-ray picture that shows the injury, then they superimpose another plate with a key number and patient's name on it, and it would take an expert to find anything wrong.

"If someone has his suspicions aroused and is specifically looking for something of the sort, it might be possible to detect the fake, but the average insurance adjuster having an attorney dig an X-ray photograph out of the files and seeing the name of the patient and all of that, is pretty much inclined to take it for granted, and if the X-ray photograph shows a real injury, the agent will settle on that kind of a basis."

"And you think this nurse has been pulling out photographs?"

"The hospital seems to think so," I said. "Apparently they'd like to get rid of her but they don't want to make an out-and-out accusation. On the other hand, the whole trouble may be due to a supervisor who doesn't like her and is trying to get rid of her.

"That's where you come in, and what we're going to be doing during the next hour. We're going out to the Bulwin Apartments and you're going to talk with the roommate, a girl named Josephine Edgar."

"You've already talked with her?" Bertha asked.

"I've already talked with her," I said, "but I didn't get anyplace. She has lots of this and that and these and those and she stood close to me and moved her body a little bit, and when I accused her of using sex, said she hadn't used sex . . . yet."

Bertha sighed and said, "That's the effect you have on all of them."

I shook my head, "Not that much of an effect," I said. "She was too impressionable, too fast. She pulled that sex stuff too fast and it was early in the morning."

"So what do I do?" Bertha asked.

"You," I said, "take her to pieces and I'll see what makes her tick."

Bertha heaved herself up out of the squeaking chair, said, "Let me powder my nose first, and I'll be with you."

She waddled over to the door and down the hall.

I walked into my office, pulled up the blotter on my desk and found the note from Elsie. It was written so that no one else would know what it meant. It said:

I told you he was horrid and I thought so until he called this afternoon and asked me to come out and meet him for a talk. Donald, he's really wonderful! He *does* understand all of the things I thought he didn't appreciate last night. I waited until late for you. I put through the telephone call you wanted, and the party I talked with said she would check on M. D. but she had heard M. D. had checked out. She was going to find out about it and said you could call her this evening. If there's anything I can do for you, call me. Elsie.

I folded the note, put it in my pocket and waited for Bertha.

Chapter 12

We pulled up in front of the Bulwin Apartments.

Bertha looked the place over, said, "Pretty classy dump for a couple of working gals, if you ask me."

"I didn't ask you," I said. "I brought you."

Bertha heaved herself out of the car and we walked into the place and went up to Apartment 283.

Luck was with us. Josephine Edgar was home.

"Why, hello, Donald," she said with syrup dripping from her voice and then turned to look at Bertha.

I said, "Miss Edgar, I want to present Bertha Cool. She's my partner. She wants to talk with you."

Bertha didn't say a word. She just pushed forward, and Josephine gave ground in order to keep from being trampled.

Bertha barged on into the room, looked around and then turned to me. "What about it?" she asked me.

I said, "I want to find out about Melita Doon."

Josephine said with something of a panic in her voice, "I told you everything I knew this morning, Donald.

"As far as I know, Melita Doon is a perfectly respectable young woman. She's working hard trying to support her invalid mother, and I resent having you come barging into the apartment this way."

"Resent and be damned," Bertha said, "but if you think you're going to pull that line of crap with a professional investigator, you're crazy as hell."

"What do you mean?" Josephine asked.

"This business about the poor little girl supporting her mother and trying to get along as best she can," Bertha said. "Take a look at this dump, it costs money. No two girls can afford this on the type of money you make—particularly if they're supporting invalid mothers.

"Where the hell is Melita's bedroom?"

Josephine was speechless, she simply gestured toward a door.

"Then this one must be yours?" Bertha said.

"That's right."

Bertha started walking toward Josephine's bedroom.

"Here, you, come out of there!" Josephine said.

Bertha kept right on walking.

Josephine ran and grabbed Bertha and tugged.

Bertha gave a sidearm swipe and sent Josephine spinning across the apartment.

Bertha walked in through the open door, started looking through closets.

"Who do these men's clothes belong to?" Bertha asked.

"You . . . you . . . you get out of here! I'm going to call the police."

Bertha tossed a couple of men's suits out on the bed, looked in the inside breast pockets for a tailor's label, picked a shirt from a drawer and noted the neat letter C embroidered on the breast pocket.

"You must think a lot of that guy," Bertha said.

"That's my cousin," Josephine said defiantly. "He left some things here while he was gone on a trip."

Bertha Cool prowled around the bedroom, then walked back into the living room, went into the other bedroom, prowled around, came back and said, "What the hell's the idea?"

"What idea?"

"Stealing X rays."

"She wasn't stealing X rays!" Josephine said. "I tell you it's that supervisor."

"This Doon girl got a boy friend?" Bertha asked.

"No, absolutely not!"

"Baloney," Bertha said.

She came walking back and said to me, "She's being subsidized in a big way."

Josephine said, "I don't know what redress I have in a matter of this kind, but I'm certainly going to see my lawyer. I think I can have your license revoked. You have no right to come in here and make an unauthorized search."

Bertha said, "That's right, dearie. You go ahead and complain to the authorities and we'll find out who this mysterious cousin of yours is and— Let's see if he has a wife."

Bertha walked over to the bed and began an expert appraisal of the suits of clothes.

"Here's a cleaning tag," she said. "Donald, take this number down. C436128.

"Well," Bertha said, turning toward the door, "I guess that's all we can do here. These babes are pretty well set up."

Josephine started to cry.

"You can't use that evidence," she said. "You simply can't. That cleaning tag, that—"

"Yes, yes, I know," Bertha said soothingly, "your cousin— Well, we won't make any fuss about things unless you start making a fuss."

Bertha pushed her way over to the door.

I followed her out.

In the hall, I said, "Good heavens, Bertha, you took chances that time. You had no right going into that bedroom."

"Forget it," Bertha said. "These women hypnotize you. I can tell a phony as far as I can see one."

"Phonies are sometimes the ones that file the big lawsuits," I said.

"I know," Bertha said, "but those girls are vulnerable. They've got a racket. What kind of a babe is this Melita Doon?"

We crowded into the elevator and I said, "She's rather a subdued choir girl who doesn't use any sex."

"Baloney," Bertha said. "She either uses sex or she's

selling X-ray pictures like mad. Her clothes may look simple and virtuous to you, but those were pretty damned good rags hanging in that closet.

"And don't think for a minute that Josephine is calling on her boy friend to support a double apartment that will keep Melita in style just because she likes company."

We rattled down to the ground floor. Bertha pounded her way out to the car, squeezed in, slammed the door shut so that it all but broke the glass and said, "My God, Donald, you shouldn't have wasted all my time. You should have been able to spot that setup as phony the minute you saw it.

"Sick mother!

"Sick mother, my fanny!"

I drove Bertha to her apartment, then went on out to Breckinridge's house.

I parked the car in the wide driveway, leaving room for other cars to get past, and went up the steps to the front door.

Breckinridge had the door open before I had a chance to get my finger on the bell button.

"Come in, Donald," he said cordially. "I've been trying to reach you all afternoon."

"So I understood," I said, "but I thought you had relieved us of all responsibility in the case, so I didn't bother to check—"

"I made a big mistake, Donald," he said, "and I'm going to be the first to acknowledge it."

161

I followed him into the living room. "All right," I said, "what's cooking?"

"I have received a report from Arizona," he said.

"You sent an agent down?" I asked.

"I didn't," he said. "I received a telephone call and as a result of that call I felt certain that it would be worse than useless to send any agent out to try and effect a settlement at this time."

"How come?"

"Well, to begin with I am afraid that after a person works a clever scheme once or twice it doesn't pay to try to work it after that."

I waited for him to go on.

"Sit down, Lam. Make yourself comfortable. Would you care for a little Scotch and soda, or a little bourbon and Seven-up?"

"I'm fine," I told him. "We may not have much time to talk frankly, so we'd better go into things while the going is good."

"Yes, indeed," Breckinridge said, "that's very good logic.

"Well, here's the situation, Lam. This idea of a fake contest has worked like a charm in two cases that have gone to court and in three cases that we settled. It didn't work quite as well when our operatives became intimate— I told you about that.

"But it was a fine idea. We let the claimant feel that he had won a contest which entitled him to two weeks' free vacation at the Butte Valley Guest Ranch. He would go there and when he saw the setup, he would start entering into the life. As you know, life at a guest ranch is hardly conducive to the type of rest an invalid would need.

"In no time at all, we'd have pictures of the claimant swinging golf clubs, diving into the pool, making eyes at some of the impressionable young women who were always around, and sometimes our representative there, Dolores Ferrol, would have him so completely gaga that he would be trying to stand on his head if she even indicated she'd like to see him try.

"But those cases that went to court betrayed us. Melvin evidently found out about our fake contest, our connection at the Butte Valley Guest Ranch and all the rest of it.

"So A. B. Melvin shows up all loaded for bear."

"When?"

"This morning. But I think that he had been planning to trap us. I think Bruno and he have been working hand and glove all the time."

"So what's the score now?"

"Melvin is at the guest ranch. He's found out about the murder charge against Foley Chester."

"How did that happen?"

"Simplest thing in the world," Breckinridge said. "When Melvin got in on the case, he wanted to get a line on Chester. He knew, of course, he was dealing with an insurance company but he wanted to find out about Chester.

"He evidently got in touch with the detective agency here that handles his business. They started looking up

Chester and in no time at all found out there was a police stakeout on the apartment and then got the whole story.

"That was all Melvin needed. The cat's out of the bag now. Melvin is in the saddle and he knows it. Heaven knows what kind of a settlement we'll have to make with him."

"Well, why didn't you send the insurance adjuster down to investigate the case and make the payment— if it's a fair question?" I asked.

"It's very fair," he said, "but the answer is embarrassing. Melvin had met our adjuster on a previous case, and the adjuster was no match for the attorney."

"So now what?"

"I want *you* to go down there. I've secured four cashier's checks payable to Helmann Bruno and A. B. Melvin in amounts of twenty-five thousand dollars. That's one hundred thousand dollars in cash. I think you can settle it for that."

"You're willing to go that high?"

"I'm willing to go that high if you have to—and I think you will."

I said, "This man, Melvin, has won cases through sharp practice?"

"He's clever, he's sharp, yes."

"And you think he's used faked X-ray pictures?"

"I wouldn't put it past him."

"And you still want to pay him a fancy sum to settle?"

"I want to get rid of this case. When your insured

164

is going to be indicted for murder, it puts the insurance company in an absolutely impossible position."

"And if your trained insurance adjuster couldn't handle Melvin, what makes you think I can?"

"Because," Breckinridge said, "I made it a point to find out about you, Lam."

"How did you do it?"

"I took your secretary out this afternoon and had a long talk with her. You'll find out about it sooner or later so I may as well tell you right now.

"Despite the fact I was a little abrupt last night and ordered you off the case, I understand you continued to investigate on your own.

"She tells me that you have a crooked nurse who has been stealing X-ray photographs and that you are getting a lot of material collected on her.

"I don't need to tell you, Donald, if we could get Melvin in a position where we could prove he had cut corners or used falsified photographs or anything of that sort, we'd give you the damnedest, sweetest bonus you ever had in your life—I say *we* would—I mean every insurance company operating in this part of the country would get together and give you a handsome bonus and throw you all the business your agency could possibly handle.

"I was absolutely astounded at some of the things Miss Brand told me; things about cases you've handled which demonstrate your very remarkable ability. I—"

The door of the living room opened and Mrs. Breckinridge came striding in.

I jumped to my feet. "Good evening, Mrs. Breckinridge."

"How do you do, Mr. Lam," she said. Then looking around the room, "Where's your secretary?"

I registered polite surprise at the question, and said, "Probably at home. I have my own car tonight. She had met me at the airport when I flew in from Texas."

"I see," she said, smiling, "and how's the case going?"

I smiled. "I'll have to let Mr. Breckinridge answer that. He's the general, I'm only the private."

"You're a colonel," Breckinridge said promptly, "and you're doing a wonderful job.

"Here is the envelope with the papers I spoke about. There's also a complete release in there. Now, I'd like to have you get on the first plane in the morning and go back—you understand, go back and handle this thing."

"Back where?" Mrs. Breckinridge asked.

"Dallas," I said, casually.

"You have enough money for expenses?" Breckinridge asked.

"Sure."

"Well, go ahead and use your judgment. The sky's the limit."

"And I can go up to this amount that you mentioned by way of settlement?"

"You can go beyond it if you feel the situation justifies it."

"I'll take a plane that will get me in there early so I can get to work," I told him.

"And you'll keep me posted?"

"I'll keep you posted."

Breckinridge shook hands.

Mrs. Breckinridge gave me a cordial smile. "I'm afraid my husband is working you at pretty late hours, Mr. Lam."

"Oh, it's all in the game," I told her.

"You work by yourself, or do you have a partner?"

"I have a partner," I said, "in the agency business."

"It's Cool and Lam," Breckinridge said hastily.

"And who is Mr. Cool?" she asked.

"It's Mrs. Cool."

Instantly her lips clamped together in a firm, thin line.

"Bertha Cool," I explained, "is in her sixties. She weighs around a hundred and sixty odd and she always reminds me of a spool of barbwire. She's hard and she's tough. For the most part she handles the office end of the business and I'm out on the firing line."

Mrs. Breckinridge was smiling once more. "That must make for a very efficient partnership," she said.

"It does," I told her. "Sometimes when the female sirens try to pull the wool over *my* eyes, Bertha steps into the picture and what she can do to one of those come-on cuties in about ten seconds is really something."

Mrs. Breckinridge was positively beaming. "I think that's a splendid arrangement. I'm very pleased my husband is employing your firm.

"The average man has absolutely no idea how a

woman can twist him around her fingers, particularly some of these little vampires who flaunt their physical charms in order to get what they want.

"From time to time, I try to warn my husband against some of the people who would take advantage of him. I know that he thinks I'm unduly suspicious."

"Not at all, my dear," Breckinridge hastened to say.

"I think it would be simply wonderful to have your Bertha Cool turned loose on some of these people sometimes," she said to me.

"It's really a great experience to watch her work," I said.

"What does she do?"

"Oh," I said, "Bertha is pretty rough and at times rather profane. She tells these women that they're dealing with another woman now; that tears and nylon will mean absolutely nothing. Then she proceeds to take them apart and if they want to get rough about it, Bertha can shake them until their teeth rattle. Bertha isn't a lady when she starts taking one of these vampires to pieces. Her language would shock you, Mrs. Breckinridge."

Mrs. Breckinridge's eyes were glittering. "Homer," she said, reproachfully, "you didn't tell me anything about this delightful character. How long have you been using this firm of detectives?"

"This is the first case," Breckinridge said. "We're just getting acquainted, so to speak."

"Well, I think it's wonderful," Mrs. Breckinridge said. "It sounds like a *very* fine combination. . . .

Well, I mustn't interfere with your business conversation. I'll be running along."

She gave me her hand and a cordial smile and left the room.

Breckinridge looked at me and said, "I guess Elsie Brand was right, Donald."

"What do you mean?"

"You're one damned smart individual," he said. "Now, get the hell down there and settle that Bruno case and get it out of my hair. Make the best settlement you can, but get it settled."

"On my way," I told him.

Chapter 13

Buck Kramer met me at the airport. "We're going to have to make a special rate on you," he said, grinning, "or else we'll have to arrange to come in and meet you on horseback. Seems like I've been doing nothing except driving you around."

"No other customers on this plane?" I asked.

"No other customers," he said. "We're getting pretty well filled up at that."

"You had several cabins vacant when I left."

"This is the peak of the season. They're filling up fast."

"Usual types?" I asked.

"One of them isn't."

I looked at him sharply. I had been there long enough to sense that there was a rule prohibiting the help from talking to one guest about other guests.

"How come?" I asked.

"He was interested in you," Kramer said.

"The deuce he was!"

"Well, now, wait a minute," Kramer said. "He didn't

mention you by name but he described you pretty well."

"What do you mean?"

"He asked particularly if there was some man there who had been going in to the airport to use the telephone, who didn't seem particularly interested in the life at the ranch, but was doing a lot of running around on business."

"And you told him about me?" I asked.

"Shucks, no," Kramer said. "I looked at him just as blank as a sheet of writing paper and told him the people I knew came there to relax and do riding, not to do business. I think this guy's an attorney, comes from Dallas—spends some time with this fellow who had the whiplash injury. Don't know whether it's coincidence or not, but it's a little strange he was interested in you."

I laughed and said, "Oh, he wasn't really interested in me. He was just wondering if perhaps some other attorney was on the job."

"Could be," Kramer said enigmatically, and then added, "We lost a customer yesterday. Melita Doon took off right quick. She said her mother was worse, but she took a plane for Dallas instead of Los Angeles."

"Is that so?" I said.

"Uh-huh. Mean anything to you?"

"Does it mean anything to you?" I asked.

He grinned and said, "Still water runs deep."

I said, "I'll have to settle down here a bit and pay more attention to my riding."

Kramer said, "I'm back and forth to the airport quite a bit. Any time I go, you're welcome to ride along. I like company. You're a good egg."

"Thanks," I told him.

We got out to the dirt road and turned in. Buck drove the car up to the parking area and stopped. I got up and gave him my hand. "Thanks, Buck."

"Don't mention it," he said. "I guess a guy in this job gets like a horse. He can size up a rider pretty damned fast."

I went to my cabin, washed up and decided to stroll out and see what Dolores Ferrol had to say before I tried to make any contact with Helmann Bruno.

Dolores was out on the horseback ride. She occasionally went out when there were women along who needed to be indoctrinated into the informalities of ranch life.

When I came back, a man was standing at the door of my cabin. He apparently was trying to fit a key to the spring lock on my door.

He turned to me with a friendly smile. "Seem to be having a devil of a time making this key work," he said. Then he turned back to the door, and almost in the same breath, exclaimed, "Well, no wonder! It's the wrong cabin. Now, *how* could I have been so stupid? I am not usually troubled with a lack of orientation."

I walked up on the porch.

"Good heavens, don't tell me this is *your* cabin!"

"This is my cabin."

"Well, well, well, I guess we're next-door neighbors. I'm A. B. Melvin of Dallas, the 'A. B.' standing for 'Alexis Bott.' Can you imagine parents inflicting names like that on an offspring?"

"You're an attorney, I take it, Mr. Melvin?"

"Why, that's right. How in the world did you guess that?"

"Just from your manner."

He said, "I didn't get your name."

"Lam," I told him. "Donald Lam."

He extended his hand, pumped my arm up and down with an excess of cordiality.

"You're on a vacation, I take it, Mr. Lam?"

"In a way," I said. "And you're here on business?"

"Well . . ." He paused, then grinned and said, "In a way."

"I'm right next door to you, Lam," he said, pointing to the next cabin, "and we'll probably be seeing quite a bit of each other."

"I thought that cabin over there was occupied," I said. "Miss Doon, I believe, from Los Angeles. What happened to her?"

"I don't know for sure," Melvin said, "but there was some young woman here who left rather unexpectedly —got a telegram about her mother being in serious condition or taking a turn for the worse or something.

"What did this girl look like—rather blond, slender?"

I nodded.

"I guess that's the one all right," Melvin said. "Her mother took a bad turn. She had to go back."

173

"That's a shame," I said. "I thought that she'd been having a rather tough time of it and needed a rest."

Melvin let that go as of no interest to him. "You're going to be here for a while, Lam?" he asked.

"I can't tell," I said. "How long are *you* going to be here?"

"I'm leaving," he said. "I told you my trip was partially on business. I've accomplished what I wanted and I'll be leaving before too very long, but I have an idea we'll see a good deal of each other."

I said, "How would you like to quit sparring around and put your cards on the table?"

"Okay by me," he said. "How's Homer?"

"Homer?" I asked.

"Breckinridge," he said. "All Purpose Insurance Company. Quite a guy."

I unlocked the door. "Come in," I invited.

Melvin followed me in. "It took me a little while to get you spotted," he said, "but once I got you spotted I didn't have any trouble running you down. Donald Lam, the firm of Cool and Lam, private detectives. Breckinridge is working on a new angle this time; before he's used company adjusters and investigators. This time he's gone out and hired an independent agency."

"Sit down," I said. "Make yourself comfortable. Tell me more about Breckinridge. You interest me."

"I thought I would. Breckinridge is quite a guy. Dignified, likes to be the big executive type. Married money. His wife's the principal stockholder in the All Purpose Insurance Company. Quite an interesting person, his wife.

"That's a good insurance company, however. They're making quite a bit of money, and I guess Breckinridge manages things all right, but he holds his office dependent on his wife's pleasure."

"Are you telling me that for some particular reason?" I asked.

"Sure, I am. You said you wanted to put the cards on the table, I'll *put* cards on the table.

"Breckinridge had a pretty slick idea. He'd stage a phony contest. Persons who were making claims against the insurance company would win that contest. The prize they'd win would be two weeks' vacation at this place.

"The woman who runs it, Shirley Gage, doesn't have any idea what it's being used for. Dolores Ferrol is the connecting link—some link—some connection!

"Boy, oh boy, if Homer Breckinridge's wife found out about *that* setup! She knows there's something doing down here and that Breckinridge has a female operative, but she doesn't know anything at all about the details."

"Details?" I asked.

"Got half an hour?" Melvin asked.

"Sure," I said. "However, mind you, I haven't said anything yet. You're doing the talking."

"Of course I am," Melvin said. "I'm going to do

enough talking so that you'll *have* to talk. Then you can go ring up Breckinridge for authorization and we'll make a settlement."

"Settlement of what?"

"The Helmann Bruno claim. What did you think?"

"You're representing him?"

Melvin laughed. "Of course I'm representing him, and I have been from the time of the accident.

"When Bruno came to me and told me about winning this contest," he said, "it was so darned easy he thought there might be something phony about it."

"What did you think?"

"I didn't have to think. I knew! Breckinridge has made three or four settlements on account of stuff he's been able to do at this place. He's blasted the claimants in two lawsuits all to hell. That should be enough. The damned fool should have quit while the quitting was good, and thought up something new, but he kept working the same old gag.

"I was in court on one of those damage suits, sitting in the audience. I had a tip-off that the insurance company was going to blast the claimant and I wanted to see how they did it.

"It was a pretty slick piece of work. The fellow was claiming he had a slipped disc and they had pictures of him showing off in front of a couple of women here at the swimming pool, doing fancy dives and then they had pictures of him on the golf course.

"By the time they got through showing those pictures, the plaintiff had collapsed. His attorney virtually threw in the sponge. The jury returned a verdict within fifteen minutes—found in favor of the defendant, of course.

"So when Bruno told me he'd won a prize, a two-week vacation out here at the Butte Valley Guest Ranch, I told him to go right ahead and take the vacation. Just to be careful not to overdo physically."

Melvin closed his right eye in a wink.

"I just wanted to see what happened *this* time. I gave Bruno an opportunity to get established and thought he'd be able to tell me what was going on. But he didn't, so I came up here and found that one of the dudes was using the telephone a lot, going back and forth. His name was Donald Lam, so I checked on Donald Lam, and sure enough, found that he was a private detective.

"Now, if you'll come to my cabin with me, *I'll* show *you* some pictures."

"I'm still not saying anything," I said.

"Don't," he told me. "Just come on over."

I walked over to his cabin.

He pulled the shades, brought out a small portable motion-picture projector and a screen.

"This isn't quite as good a job as the insurance company did in those other cases," he said, "but they had screened cameras, long focal-length lenses and professional photographers.

"I had to buy these shots from an amateur—one of those shutterbug tourists," Melvin went on. "But you'll get a kick out of the pictures."

Melvin switched off the lights, started the camera.

There was a bright light on the screen and a flickering, then suddenly colored motion pictures, small but distinct, came to life.

Homer Breckinridge was in a swimming suit and lounging by the pool, looking up at Dolores Ferrol who was seated by the pool, one foot dangling in the water.

Breckinridge was lounging on one elbow.

He said something that caused her to laugh. She leaned forward, dipped one hand in the water, held it up and snapped the fingers, sending drops of cold water on Breckinridge's face.

He made a grab for her. She tried to elude him but didn't get up quite fast enough. He caught an ankle, pulled her to him, then switched from the ankle to the leg. He held her down, reached his hand down into the swimming pool then came up with a cupped palm full of water.

She talked him out of it, lying there looking up at him smiling, her legs across his lap.

Slowly, he moved his cupped palm back over the swimming pool, opened it, shook the water out of it and wiped his hand off on his bathing trunks.

Then he patted Dolores on the bare leg.

She squirmed seductively, getting up away from his lap and to her feet.

Breckinridge got up and walked away with her.

The camera showed them walking over toward the main house. Breckinridge put his hand on her shoulder, then let it slide down and gave her a little pat on the fanny.

The motion pictures flickered off, sputtered for a moment then came on with another scene.

This was a twilight scene. The illumination wasn't so good here. The figures were mostly silhouetted but it was possible to recognize Breckinridge and Dolores.

They were talking earnestly over by the corrals. Apparently they had just come in from a ride. Dolores was dressed in a tight-fitting riding outfit, and Breckinridge was wearing Pendletons and a five-gallon sombrero, looking like the dashing cowpuncher.

Dolores said something to him, then reached up and took his hat, took it from his head and put it on her own, tilting it up. She tilted her chin up and looked at him. Her manner was challenging.

Breckinridge grabbed her and kissed her, then they melted together into one dark blotch.

"Light wasn't very good on that one," Melvin explained. "I believe it was actually a few minutes after sunset."

The screen flickered again, then a scene of a breakfast ride came on. Breckinridge swung awkwardly off his horse. Dolores, supple and graceful, came down from the saddle.

Breckinridge took her arm with a proprietary air, piloted her over to the chuck wagon. They had coffee, then ham and eggs. They were talking earnestly.

When they had finished, Breckinridge extended his hand. Dolores took it. They shook hands, then walked away down over to where the horses were standing. They walked around a horse, stood for a moment with the horse screening them from the rest of the party.

The camera flickered off.

"Getting a new camera angle," Melvin said. "This will be good."

The camera came on again. The photographer had apparently managed to move around so the picture showed the other side of the horse, showed Breckinridge and Dolores standing there. This time, Breckinridge took her in his arms with tenderness. They clung to each other for some ten seconds, then separated hastily as one of the wranglers came walking into view past the horse's rear.

Melvin shut off the camera and started reversing the film.

"More?" I asked.

"It gets boring after a while," Melvin said. "This will give you the idea. This motion-picture business is something two people can play at."

"And just what do you intend to do with those pictures?" I asked.

"That's up to you," he said.

"What do you mean?"

"These pictures," Melvin said, "are part of Bruno's case."

"How come?"

"Oh, it's just the way I propose to handle it," Melvin said. "I'm not certain that I can get all this introduced in evidence as being pertinent, but my idea is to try to show the fact that the insurance company, instead of trying to minimize the damages and lessen my client's pain and suffering, was actually trying to exaggerate them by putting him in a position where he'd be inclined to overdo, to overexert himself and to violate the doctor's instructions.

"In order to show that, I'm going to prove that this whole dude ranch business is a trap maintained by the insurance company for the purpose of getting people to overexert and overextend themselves.

"I'm going to put on quite a little story. First, I'm going to show Breckinridge getting acquainted with Dolores Ferrol, then I'm going to take Breckinridge's deposition and ask him if he didn't reach an agreement with Dolores by which she was to act as representative of the insurance company and use her sex appeal to get these people to try to show how masculine they were, and all that stuff.

"Of course, I'll be frank with you, Lam, I'm not certain that I can get away with having all this stuff in evidence. It has to be on the theory that instead of offering treatment to the injured, the company actually engaged in a conspiracy to try and get him to do things that would damage his case in front of a jury, but which, at the same time, would enhance his injuries.

"For instance, yesterday while you were gone, Dolores was making quite a play for Bruno. She got him up out of his wheelchair a couple of times and got him to walk down to the corrals with her. That was contrary to the doctor's orders and against my instructions. He's not supposed to be walking over rough ground without a cane. The girl's clever.

"Bruno told me that afterwards when he got back to his cabin he had quite a dizzy spell. Now, as far as I'm concerned that constitutes an aggravation of injury by the insurance company.

"Anyway, this reel of motion pictures is not intended to be used except as a part of my case. I wouldn't use it personally to embarrass Breckinridge for anything on earth."

"It would be blackmail if you did," I pointed out.

"Provided I wanted anything for it, it would be blackmail," he corrected me, "but I'm only using it in connection with Bruno's case. As Bruno's attorney, I'm entitled to use it."

"What you're trying to tell me," I said, "is that once the case is settled you'll give me a complete release from Bruno and turn the reel of motion pictures over to me."

"Right."

"How much?"

"A hundred grand," he said.

"You're way, way, way off," I told him. "No questionable whiplash injury is going to be settled for a hundred grand."

"Suit yourself," he told me. "I'd just as soon go to court over it. I think I have a good case."

"Well, you're not going to get any hundred thousand settlement," I told him.

"You're a pretty cocky young fellow," he said. "Before you make any final statements like that, you'd better talk with Homer Breckinridge.

"When I sue, I'm going to sue for two hundred and fifty thousand and I'm going to file suit within the next forty-eight hours, and as part of my complaint I'm going to allege that, as a result of a conspiracy on the part of the insurance company, my client had his injuries aggravated.

"And I'm just mentioning that it won't do you any good to try and contact Bruno independently, because Bruno is leaving when I leave."

"Going back to Dallas?" I asked.

"I don't think so," Melvin said, smiling. "I think he'll be someplace where it would be difficult to reach him until after the suit has been filed and he has been interviewed by the press."

I said, "All right, now *I'm* going to talk."

"Go right ahead," Melvin said.

I said, "You're an attorney. You can represent your client but you can't resort to blackmail. Now, you are trying to blackmail Breckinridge into paying an exorbitant amount by way of settlement in order to get those motion pictures back."

Melvin apparently became enraged. "What the hell are you talking about," he said, "accusing me of blackmail!"

"If it weren't for those pictures you wouldn't set any such figure by way of settlement."

"Oh, is that so!" he said. "Well, you're so damned smart perhaps you don't know that your client is being sought for murder right now by the Los Angeles police."

"What?" I asked.

"That's a fact," he said. "Check on it. I wasn't supposed to let the cat out of the bag, but since you're talking blackmail to me, I'll talk murder to you.

"Your man, Chester, that the insurance company is representing, had been having trouble with his wife for a while.

"In the days when they had a happier marriage and they wanted to take care of property rights, they took out a joint insurance policy in the amount of a hundred grand. But after the romance went on the rocks and Chester got the idea his wife was cheating on him, he wound up having one big fight with her and she walked out on him. He followed her from their apartment to San Bernardino; from San Bernardino she was driving to San Francisco, and he followed her and pushed her off the road. He was after that insurance.

"Unfortunately the car didn't roll as far as Chester had expected, so he cracked his wife over the noggin with a jack handle, pushed the car down to the bottom of the barranca, and set it on fire."

"Where do you get all that?" I asked.

He said, "I have connections with the police in Dallas. The Los Angeles police found that Chester was mixed up in an accident in Dallas and wanted to know all about it, and wanted particularly to know if the man who was injured had any address for Chester that would help locate him.

"So the police came to me to find out whether Bruno had any address different from what the Los Angeles police had, and I made them tell me what they were working on before I consented even to get in touch with Bruno, which I did by telephone yesterday.

"Now then, you tell Breckinridge that when this case comes up for trial we're going to be suing for two hundred and fifty thousand dollars, that we're going to claim the insurance company aggravated my client's injuries, that we're going to try a few motion pictures of our own, and that the jurors are going to know that the man we're suing is either a fugitive from justice or is awaiting trial on a charge of murdering his wife.

"Now then, you laugh that off and don't go telling me a hundred grand is too much to ask by way of settlement in a case of *that* sort."

"Where will you be?" I asked.

"I can be reached at my office in Dallas," he said. "And any time anyone wants to reach Helmann Bruno, he can be reached through me. In the meantime, he won't be available to sign any papers or make any statements.

"I imagine you'll want to telephone Breckinridge confidentially from a telephone booth, probably at the airport, so I'm giving you forty-eight hours within which to arrange a settlement."

Melvin shot out his hand. "Awfully nice meeting you, Lam," he said. "The fact that we're on opposite sides of the case doesn't need to affect our pleasant relationship. . . . You'll be leaving, I take it, before Dolores gets back?"

"I'll be leaving," I told him.

"And I don't think you'll be back," he said, smiling. "I'll say good-by to her for you."

"Do that," I told him.

I went back and hunted up Buck Kramer. "How about a rush trip to the airport?" I asked.

"Again?" he asked.

"Again," I told him.

"Why don't you get them to furnish one of the sleeping bags that we have for outdoor camping and spread it out there in the foyer of the airport?"

"I think I will," I told him. "As a matter of fact, I may not be back here."

His face lost its grin. "Any trouble, Lam?" he asked.

"A little," I said.

"That lawyer from Dallas?"

"He's connected with it."

"Say the word," he said, "and I'll have that lawyer immobilized."

I raised my eyebrows.

"Oh no," Kramer said, "nothing crude, you understand. I wouldn't stand for anything like that, and I wouldn't expose Mrs. Gage to any suit or even any criticism. In fact, it would be done so smoothly that this damned lawyer wouldn't even know what had happened to him."

"Just by way of curiosity," I asked, "what *would* happen to him?"

"Well," Kramer said, "you say the word and I'll take him out on a most interesting ride. I'll see that he has the right sort of a horse."

"You wouldn't have him bucked off?" I asked.

"Heaven forbid!" Kramer said. "But we have a few horses that are pretty stiff in the shoulders and when they trot—well, I'll tell you it takes a damned good rider to sit a trot on one of those horses; and because they're slow walkers, they'd rather trot than walk.

"So when we have someone who's particularly obstreperous— Hell, Lam, I shouldn't be telling you this. I'm letting you in on a lot of secrets."

"They're secrets, as far as I'm concerned," I told him. "I'm just interested, that's all."

"Well, we put them on one of those rough horses and put some fast-walking horses in the string, and those stiff horses trot every damned step of the way, and by the time the dude gets back he isn't feeling like doing any dancing for a little while."

I said, "Buck, I'm representing an insurance company. I've been told to pay out anything that is necessary or advisable for expenses. I think you're entitled to a hundred bucks, and as far as I'm concerned, I would like very much to have Alexis Bott Melvin immobilized to some extent."

"It'll be done," Kramer said. "I have some interesting things to show him. Under the circumstances, you won't mind if one of the other fellows drives you in to the airport, because this is a deal I'll have to handle myself."

"I won't mind in the least," I said, "if someone else drives me in to the airport."

We shook hands.

"Come back any time," Kramer said. "It's nice to have you here, Lam. I like to work with people who get along with horses."

He turned and called one of the wranglers. "Get the station wagon," he said, "and take Mr. Lam in to the airport right away, will you?"

"Right away," the wrangler said.

Chapter 14

I called Breckinridge from the airport.

"You're reporting early," Breckinridge said. "I take it that you have good news, Lam, that you have everything all settled and that congratulations are in order."

"Congratulations are a trifle premature," I said.

"You mean you *didn't* settle it?"

"No."

"What's the trouble this time?"

I said, "I can't discuss it in detail over the telephone. I take it this call is going through a switchboard?"

"What difference does that make?"

"It may be monitored."

"I have no secrets in regard to company business," Breckinridge said. "You go right ahead and tell me anything you have to tell me."

I said, "If it's not impertinent, Mr. Breckinridge, who made the initial contact here at the ranch with the person who was to represent the insurance company?"

"That doesn't enter into it at all," he said.

"Have you been here at the ranch, personally?"

189

"I was there personally on a vacation at one time," he said coldly, "and I fail to see what that has to do with it."

I said, "Melvin located some of the people who were there at the ranch at the same time you were. He located one woman in particular who had a small motion-picture camera and took motion pictures of about everything in sight. He has motion pictures of you and one other person."

There was deep, shocked silence at the other end of the line.

"You there?" I asked.

"I'm here," Breckinridge said.

I said, "Melvin intends to use those pictures as part of his case."

"Good God!" Breckinridge said.

I said, "This Melvin impresses me as being rather a dangerous antagonist and quite unscrupulous."

"Unscrupulous is no name for it," Breckinridge said. "He can't be bluffing about those pictures, can he, Lam?"

I said, "He showed me part of the roll that he had, not all of it."

"What did it show?"

"Well, that's something I *can't* tell you over the telephone."

"Where are you now?"

"At the airport."

"Where's Bruno, at the ranch?"

"Yes, but Melvin's moving him out."

"And where's Melvin?"

"He's going to stay at the ranch today and then he's going to go to his office in Dallas tomorrow."

"Settle that case!" Breckinridge snapped. "Get in touch with him. Give him anything he wants."

I said, "We have forty-eight hours' leeway."

"All right, you have cashier's checks. I want you to effect a *complete* settlement. I want it *complete*."

"Meaning you want the motion pictures?"

"At times," Breckinridge said, "you're rather astute."

"All right," I told him, "I'll be in Dallas tonight. I'll clean things up within the forty-eight hours."

"See that you do, Lam. This is imperative."

I said, "This nurse, Melita Doon, who was staying here, seems to have left in a hurry. Her mother is supposed to have taken a turn for the worse. I don't know whether we could find her and perhaps—well, she *might* give us some information. She might be the weak link in the chain."

"Weak link, nothing!" Breckinridge said. "I want that case out of the way. Never mind looking for her, just get into Dallas and be prepared to make that settlement. . . . That damned ambulance-chasing, blackmailing—"

"Hold it," I said. "That isn't going to help."

I could hear him take a deep breath at the other end of the telephone, then he said, "Lam, I certainly appreciate the way you've handled this. I appreciate very much the way you handled yourself last night. A lot of people don't realize that when you're out to get that evidence, you have to get evidence by any means that are available and there are times when you simply have to use female operatives."

"That's right," I said. "Everybody in the business knows that."

"All right," Breckinridge said wearily. "I guess we're stuck for at least a hundred grand. You know what to do, Lam, make a *complete* settlement."

"Leave it to me," I told him.

I hung up the telephone and found there was a plane for Dallas leaving within the next thirty minutes.

Chapter 15

I arrived at Dallas right on schedule, rented a car, went to the Meldone Apartments, took the elevator to the sixth floor, walked down to 614 and rang the bell.

Mrs. Bruno answered the door. She was all dressed up.

"Hello," I said, "remember me? I'm Mr. Donald, the man who sold you the set of encyclopedias and gave you the premium."

"Oh, yes," she said, "the things are working fine, Mr. Donald."

I looked past her into the room and saw a suitcase about half packed on the couch.

I said, "I'm checking up on the account."

"You'll find that I'm good credit, Mr. Donald. We meet our obligations right on the dot and—"

"Oh, it isn't that," I told her. "That's in another department altogether. I'm in the premium department. I have the job of selecting the premiums that we give away with certain exceptional purchases. For instance, women who make purchases on their wedding anniversaries, woman who are like you and buy the hundred-thousandth set and all of that. I have to buy quite a lot of premiums and I like to find out that the ones I get are giving satisfaction."

"They did. Thank you very much. They're doing all right."

"Do you have any suggestions as to the type of premiums that women are interested in?"

"Heavens, no, you couldn't have anything better than that electric can opener and that electric blender. They've been wonderful! Simply wonderful!"

"And they're working all right?"

"Like a charm."

She hesitated, then stood to one side. "Won't you come in, Mr. Donald?"

"Thank you," I said.

She said, indicating the suitcase, "I'm going to join my husband in Montana."

"Are you indeed? Expect to be gone long?"

She said, "No, I'm just going up for a visit. He's up there on a business trip. He telephoned me to ask if I wanted to join him."

"That's splendid," I said. "When are you leaving?"

"Oh, I don't know," she said. "Sometime tomorrow. I'll have to check with him again about planes. He's going to call me later on."

"I see," I told her. "Now, there's another small premium that we give for people who have won their prizes and who can give us testimonials about the encyclopedia. These are short testimonials and you get a hundred dollars apiece for them."

"A hundred dollars!"

"That's right. In cash," I told her. "It's pocket money for the housewife." I smiled and went on, "If we made it in a check, it would have to go on the income tax, and the husband, as the business manager, would be apt to assert a proprietary interest.

"As it is, this is just a personal matter for the woman of the house, and we pay it in the form of cash, five twenty-dollar bills."

"Well, for heaven's sake, why didn't you tell me about this before?"

"We can only afford to make this offer to a limited number of people," I said. "And, of course, it's confidential. No one is to know there was any compensation for the testimonial."

"Of course . . . and how is it handled? What do I do?"

I said, "You just have to read a little statement that we prepare, to the effect that you purchased the encyclopedias and were astounded to find how good they are. You have already become recognized as an authority on many bits of knowledge and the neighbors frequently come to you to settle disputes."

"You say I have to read it?"

"That's right. Then we put it on tape," I explained.

"Oh," she said.

"And then, of course, we put it in front of the television cameras," I went on.

"Television!"

"Yes."

"I . . . I don't think I'd care to do that, Mr. Donald."

"No?"

"No." She shook her head emphatically.

"It would only take a minute of your time, and several—"

"And where would you use it, just locally?"

"Oh," I said, "they'd probably use it all over the country, just in a spot announcement, you know, one of those little fifteen-second spot announcements that they buy on station time."

"No," she said. "I wouldn't be interested."

"Well," I told her, "thank you very much. I just wanted you to know that we didn't lose interest in our hundred-thousandth customer just because we had completed the sale."

I left the apartment.

She was looking a little thoughtful as I left.

I took up a vigil outside of the apartment.

It was an all-night vigil. She didn't come out until seven o'clock in the morning, then a taxi drew up and she came down and had the cabdriver bring down four suitcases. They were big, heavy suitcases.

She took them all down to the airport, shipped the four of them by airfreight and kept only a little overnight bag with her.

She bought a ticket to Los Angeles.

There's a knack about shadowing. If you are too anxious to be unobtrusive, you tip off your presence. If you just take it easy and are part of the scenery, it's damned seldom people notice you.

I cut a small hole in a newspaper so I could hold it up and pretend to be reading. I kept watch until the Los Angeles flight was announced.

Mrs. Bruno was on first class. I got a ticket on tourist class, went to the telegraph office, and sent a wire to Sgt. Frank Sellers, Los Angeles Police Force:

PRIVATE DETECTIVE DONALD LAM HERE ASKING QUESTIONS ABOUT NEW ANGLE ON MURDER CASE WHICH APPARENTLY YOU INVESTIGATING LOS ANGELES. LAM LEAVING FOR LOS ANGELES AMERICAN, FLIGHT 709, THIS MORNING. WHILE HERE INADVERTENTLY NEGLECTED SIGN TEN DOLLAR CHECK. WE CAN PROSECUTE ON THAT IF YOU WANT EXCUSE TO HOLD HIM.

I signed the telegram, "Sgt. Smith," sent it extra rush, then got aboard the tourist class section of the plane.

It's a wonderful thing in following a person on a plane to be in tourist class. There's a complete line of separation. The first-class people don't come back to the tourist class, and the tourist very seldom go up to the first class.

I settled back in my seat. The plane was nonstop to Los Angeles and I had nothing to do except doze and wonder how I was going to explain to Breckinridge that I had taken it on myself to violate his instructions.

We flew steadily westward, racing the shadows and, at the speed of jet transportation, seeming to almost keep up with them. The air was smooth, clear as crystal, and after we passed New Mexico, we looked down on the Arizona desert and then the Colorado River and the Imperial Valley.

I almost fancied that I could pick out the Butte Valley Guest Ranch as we flew over Arizona. Buck Kramer would be out putting saddles on the horses; Dolores Ferrol turning on the highly personalized charm, infatuating the guests.

Then we began our long, slow descent into the Los Angeles airport and landed so smoothly that it was hard to tell we had reached the ground until the braking effect of the motors made itself manifest.

I was at the head of the line in the tourist-class division, but after I got off and reached the point where the stream of passengers merged I hung back until I saw Mrs. Bruno walking along, very sedate, with eyes downcast.

Then suddenly Sgt. Sellers and a plain-clothes man came barging down the long corridor.

I hurried to catch up with Mrs. Bruno. "Well, well," I said, "you didn't tell me *you* were taking this plane!"

She turned to look at me with consternation on her face, then suddenly made up her mind to brush it off as best she could. "Oh, Mr. Donald," she said. "Well, heavens, you didn't tell *me you* were on this plane.

"I guess you were in first class," I said. "My company doesn't encourage me to travel on extra fare—"

"Okay, Pint Size," Sgt. Sellers said. "This way."

I said, "Well, well, Sergeant Sellers! Permit me to present the woman for whose murder you're trying to arrest Foley Chester. Mrs. Chester, this is a very dear friend of mine, Sergeant Sellers of the local police."

She looked as though she wanted to run, and that look was the thing that undid her. If she had been just a little scornful, just a little defiant and said, "What in the world are you trying to pull?" Sellers might have let her get away with it. But that look of panic gave everything away.

"What the hell are *you* talking about, Pint Size?" Sellers said, but his eyes were on the woman.

I said, "Mrs. Foley Chester, alias Mrs. Helmann Bruno."

Sellers did a double take, fished a photograph out of his pocket, and said, "I'll be god-damned if it isn't."

Then was when she started to run.

Sellers and the plainclothesman grabbed her.

By this time a crowd of gawking passengers were gathering around, and Sellers and the plainclothesman were rough with them. "On your way, folks," Sellers said. "Break it up. Keep moving. That's a lawful order from an officer. If you disobey it you'll be arrested. Either keep moving about your business or get a free ride to headquarters in the paddy wagon, whichever you want."

That started them scattering like startled chickens.

Sellers and the plainclothesman led the woman down

to one of the deserted loading rooms which they used as an interrogation room.

"All right," Sellers said, "come clean."

"Well," she said, "there's no use denying it. You've caught me."

Sellers looked at me. I said, "It had to be that way. Chester didn't push his wife over the grade on that detour, and Melita Doon, the nurse, didn't have all of her trouble because she stole a couple of X-ray pictures for a malingerer. What bothered her was the fact that she had stolen a corpse."

"A corpse?" Sellers said.

"Sure. Read the hospital report. A woman patient of Melita Doon's was supposed to have got up and walked out. She was a patient who was in for treatment in connection with an automobile accident. She died in the night.

"Chester, alias Bruno, had been waiting for a chance at a corpse like that. Melita had been stealing X rays. This time they wanted a corpse. They had been waiting for weeks for the right sort of a death on Melita's floor. They wanted an unattached woman of about Mrs. Chester's build.

"They smuggled this woman's body out of the hospital; took her clothes; clothed the body in Mrs. Chester's clothes, had Melita Doon report a walkout, and then they planted the body and burned it past recognition so Chester could collect insurance on his wife.

"Unfortunately, however, the police were a little too

efficient. They examined the rented car Chester had, found where the paint had been scraped when they pushed the other car sidewise over the grade so it would look convincing, and Chester knew that part of the jig was up. Chester and his wife had a getaway all planned. They had established secondary identities as Bruno and wife in Dallas.

"And Chester had still another ace in the hole. As Bruno, he reported an accident, a purely synthetic and imaginative accident. As Bruno, he reported that a car bearing Foley Chester's license number had bumped him from the rear and had given him a whiplash injury.

"Then he flew to Los Angeles, and as Foley Chester reported the accident to the insurance company, stating that it was all his fault and putting the insurance company in a position where they had to admit liability.

"Originally, that had been all there was to it. They'd have settled for some ten or fifteen thousand, but when you entered the picture and started making Chester a fugitive from justice, Bruno saw his real chance. He then hired an attorney to represent him so that the case could be settled without Bruno having to appear or do anything other than sign papers.

"Taken all in all, it was a sweet two-way fraud.

"The payoff was those tracks down the sandy wash.

"After Chester went down and set fire to that car, he wasn't going to climb all the way back up the hill, so he had his accomplice, who happened to be the woman he was supposed to have murdered, drive the car down to the foot of the grade. He then walked down the sandy wash.

"This guy, Chester, has been working a sweet racket. You'll find he had two accomplices, Melita Doon and Josephine Edgar. He was playing Santa Claus for them in their apartment. They stole X-ray photographs for him and then when he wanted to hit the jackpot and had Melita sucked into the fraud scheme so there was no way out for her, he had her steal a corpse.

"If you go down to their apartment in the Bulwin Apartments you'll find some of Chester's clothes there, even a shirt with a neat little C embroidered on the pocket."

Sellers had been looking at me while I was talking. From time to time he shifted his eyes to the woman. When she began to cry, Sellers knew that he'd struck pay dirt.

"All right, madam," he said, "I guess you're going to have to go to headquarters. If you have the carfare, we'll take a cab and that won't attract quite so much attention."

"Want me to go?" I asked Sellers.

Sellers jerked his thumb toward the door, "Scram," he said.

I could tell then he was already thinking of the interview he was going to give to the reporters describing the brilliant detective work by which he had uncovered the fraud.

I didn't bother to call Breckinridge. For one thing

there wasn't time. There was a night plane leaving for Dallas and I had to make it. I'd make my report to Breckinridge all in a lump.

I traveled first class this time. The hostess had made the trip in from Dallas, now she was flying back. She looked at me curiously but she didn't say anything and I didn't.

I settled back and got some sleep. I'd been up all night watching that apartment house.

I got back to Dallas, picked up my rented car and drove to Melvin's offices.

Melvin was waiting for me. It was a magnificent suite of offices with a huge law library which doubtless furnished him the tools he needed in winning cases, but also was designed to impress clients.

And he had one of his secretaries working overtime, a girl in a suit that fitted her all over.

She pressed a buzzer, and Melvin himself came out of his private office to escort me in. The guy was so sore and stiff he could hardly walk, but he tried to keep a breezy air of cordial informality.

"Hello, Lam. Hello!" he said. "How are you? I got your wire saying you'd be in on this plane so I waited. . . . Come in, come right in. I take it you're prepared to close up this case of Bruno versus Chester."

I smiled at him and said, "I think I have everything I need."

"That's fine. Sit down. Sit right down, Lam. There's no reason you and I can't be friends—after all, business is business, and an insurance company expects to pay out money. That is why it collects premiums. Their troubles are not our troubles. I'm representing a client. You're representing a client.

"You know, Lam, we have a good deal of business scattered around the country and quite frequently we have to run down witnesses in Los Angeles and get statements. I'm very glad I met you. I'm satisfied we can be a lot of help to each other."

"That's fine," I told him.

"You have the checks?" he asked, looking at my briefcase.

"I have the checks," I told him. "Do you have the motion pictures?"

He smiled and took a circular tin container out of his desk drawer. He put it on his desk, and said, "We'll settle everything all at once, Lam."

I said, "Now, these checks are payable both to A. B. Melvin, as attorney, and Helman Bruno, as the claimant."

"That's right. That's right," he said, smiling. "That's the way to do it. I like to deal with an insurance company that protects the attorney. Of course, we can always accompany our client to the bank, but it's a lot more dignified to have the client sign and then the attorney signs and the lawyer's secretary takes the checks down to the bank."

"Well," I said, "that's the way the checks are made, but I don't think you'll want them that way."

"Why not?"

"Because," I said, "if you sign them you'll be signing yourself into the penitentiary."

His face lost its cordiality and became hard and ominous.

"Now, look, Lam," he said, "I've been dealing with you straight across the board. I don't want you to try any smart double cross, because if you do I'll make you and that insurance company so damned sick, neither one of you will ever get well."

"I'm not trying any double cross," I said, with a look of candid innocence on my face. "It's your client who did that."

"What do you mean?"

I said, "Helmann Bruno *is* Foley Chester."

"What!" he exclaimed.

"And," I said, "I think an investigation will show that Chester, alias Bruno, or Bruno, alias Chester, has been making a living out of malingering for a long time. He has quite a racket. He takes out an insurance policy, then he goes to another city, establishes a double identity, reports an imaginary accident, claims that the insured is in the wrong and then, as the insured, goes to the insurance company in the city where he has his alter home and confesses that it was all his fault.

"After that, he gets some attorney and they rig up a case with the aid of stolen X-ray photographs, the insurance company makes the settlement and then they move on to their next victim."

Melvin's jaw dropped. "You're *sure* about this?"

I said, "The police arrested Mrs. Bruno this morning. It turns out she's Mrs. Foley Chester, the woman that the authorities thought had been murdered.

"This time they used the nurse, not to steal X-ray photographs, but to steal a corpse. Then they dressed this corpse in Mrs. Chester's clothes, set fire to the body and were prepared to collect a hundred thousand life insurance if they could, and, if they couldn't, they were still going to keep their racket going of bilking the insurance companies on settlements of ten, fifteen and twenty thousand dollars."

"You're sure?" he asked. "You have proof of all this?"

I said, "You have a connection with the police force here. Get them to ring up Sergeant Sellers in Los Angeles and find out about the latest developments in the Chester case."

Melvin pushed back his chair. "Excuse me a minute," he said. "I want to see my secretary about something."

He was gone about ten minutes; when he came back he was trembling.

"Lam," he said, "I want to assure you on my professional honor that I had absolutely no inkling of all this. I was acting in the highest good faith."

"Yes?" I asked.

"Yes," he said.

I motioned toward the circular tin case with the motion pictures, on his desk.

"What about those pictures?" I asked.

He looked at them, took a deep breath. I could see his

mind working. "Pictures?" he said, vacantly. "Are those pictures?"

"They seem to be."

"It's news to me. I've never seen them before. You must have brought them in."

"I'm taking them out," I told him.

I took the case, put it in my briefcase, and said, "Well, as you remarked earlier, it's all in a day's game. We're each representing a client."

"I make it a rule never to represent a crook," Melvin said. "This is a shock to me. A great shock."

"Where did you think those X-ray pictures were coming from?" I asked.

"My client had them taken."

"You didn't ask to interview the doctor?"

"I— Well, I've been terribly busy," Melvin said, lamely. "Of course, when it came time to prepare for trial, I would have investigated, but— You know, how those things are, Lam."

"I know how those things are," I said, and walked out.

Chapter 16

A midnight plane got me back to Los Angeles so I was at Breckinridge's office by the time it opened.

Breckenridge came in, looking worried. There were puffs under his eyes and his usual jaunty appearance had vanished. There was nothing crisp or youthful about him now. He had all the snap of a wilted lettuce leaf.

He registered surprise when he saw me there.

"Lam!" he exclaimed. "What are *you* doing here? You were supposed to be making a settlement in Dallas."

"I've made it."

"You've done what?"

"I've made it."

"Did you get . . . everything?"

I said, "You have a projection room here, don't you?"

He hesitated, then said, "Well, yes, but I don't want to have one of the projectionists run any pictures you have."

"I'll run them," I said.

"You know how?"

"Yes."

We went to a projection room. Breckinridge saw the pictures. When we came out, he was shaking like a leaf.

I handed him the roll of films. "You'll know what to do with those," I said.

"How much did it cost?" he asked.

"Well," I said, "I've had quite a few expenses. I've been riding back and forth between here and Dallas on the jet planes. The hostesses think I'm a company representative and—"

"Oh, that!" he said, waving his hand. "We don't give a damn about expenses. How much did you settle for?"

"Nothing," I told him.

"Nothing!"

"That's right."

"How did that happen?"

I said, "If you'll read the noon papers you'll find an article in there about how the extreme devotion of duty of Sergeant Frank Sellers, and Jim Dawson of the Sheriff's Office in Kern County, solved one of the most perplexing murder cases the state has ever had to contend with.

"At first the case seemed to be a typical accidental death. Probing deeper these veteran officers found evidence of a murder for insurance, but since one or two seemingly trivial facts didn't fit into the framework, they kept plugging away on a day-and-night basis until they uncovered a plot so bizarre that it once more proves the old adage that truth is stranger than fiction."

Breckinridge said, "Do you mean to say those two . . . gentlemen . . . took *all* of the credit in the press?"

"Sure," I said. "Why wouldn't they?"

Breckinridge said, "That is unfair. I am not entirely without influence in police circles. One of the police commissioners is my close personal friend, and I . . ."

He suddenly hesitated, and I said, ". . . While you have problems of your own."

He fingered the round can holding the motion-picture film. "While I," he echoed, "have problems of my own. But if I can't make it up to you in one way, I will in another, Lam—I not only have a bonus for you from my company but by this time tomorrow I'll have a bonus from a dozen companies that will surprise you. This man, Melvin, has been a thorn in our side for a long time."

Breckinridge went out into the outer office and came back with a check.

I looked at it, whistled, put the check in my pocket.

Breckinridge thrust out his hand, "Lam," he said, "this was a real pleasure. A *real* pleasure."

I let it go at that.

Chapter 17

I walked into the office. Bertha blinked her eyes and said, "My God, can't you ever stay in one place? How are you going to get a job finished if you keep flitting back and forth?"

"The job's finished," I told her.

Bertha said angrily, "You were supposed to have three weeks to work on it. Three weeks at sixty dollars a day is—"

I interrupted to toss Breckinridge's check on the desk in front of her.

She unfolded the check, started to say something, then her eyes began to get big.

"Fry me for an oyster," she said. And then after a moment, added, "And to think that somebody else was paying all the expenses."

"All except one five-hundred-dollar item," I said.

"A five-hundred-dollar item? What's that for?" she asked.

"A bonus for Elsie Brand," I said, and walked out of the office while she was still sputtering.